CLASSIC HORSE STORIES

Edited by Karen L. Mitchell
Illustrated by Michele Maltseff

Lowell House
Juvenile
Los Angeles

CONTEMPORARY BOOKS
Chicago

ISBN: 1-56565-231-2

Library of Congress Catalog Card Number: 94-42092

Publisher: Jack Artenstein
General Manager, Juvenile Division: Elizabeth D. Wood
Editorial Director: Brenda Pope-Ostrow
Director of Publishing Services: Rena Copperman
Project Editor: Barbara Schoichet
Managing Editor, Juvenile Division: Chris Hemesath
Art Director: Lisa-Theresa Lenthall
Typesetting: Laurie Young

Lowell House books can be purchased at special discounts when ordered in bulk for premiums and
special sales. Contact Department VH at the following address:
Lowell House Juvenile
2029 Century Park East, Suite 3290
Los Angeles, CA 90067

Manufactured in the United States of America

10 9 8 7 6 5 4 3 2 1

CONTENTS

Dear Reader:

What animal most embodies spirit, power, beauty, grace, freedom, speed, and companionship? What animal has appeared not only throughout literature, but in movies and on television as well?

The horse.

Rising from its unpretentious beginning, *Equus caballus*, as the species was first known when it was only ten to twenty inches tall, rose out of central Asia to become the noble steed that has carried warriors off to battle, cowboys across prairies, and gods and goddesses toward their heavenly destinies. Revered in Stone Age carvings and immortalized by artists ranging from Leonardo da Vinci to Picasso, horses have become American celebrities.

But whether they're just taking minor parts in westerns or starring in television classics such as *Mr. Ed*, *Fury*, or *My Friend Flicka*, horses have always proved themselves to be devoted friends to the humans who love them. And, with classic films being made from such timeless masterpiece novels as *The Black Stallion*, *Black Beauty*, and *National Velvet*, these elegant animals have warmed the hearts of past generations and will surely continue to do so for generations to come.

More than mere transportation, horses, with their sleek coats and flowing manes, have mesmerized us in enchanting myths about winged chargers pulling chariots through the sky, and inspiring legends about brave stallions herding wild mustangs across the Great Plains. When tamed, they have rescued their masters from terrible peril, and been the loyal companions to cowboys on long cattle drives. Humans, then, in return for their horses' never-ending devotion, have smuggled crisp apples and lumps of sugar into cold stables, searched relentlessly when their beloved steeds were stolen by shrewd horse thieves, and comforted their faithful friends when they lay ill on soft hay.

Whether ridden by rugged cowboys on western ranges, by victorious jockeys around splendid racetracks, or by happy children exploring dusty trails, horses have always shared our passion for wondrous adventure. Now, here in *Classic Horse Stories*, let's awaken the unbroken spirit of the stallions, mustangs, Arabians, Appaloosas, palominos, pintos, and ponies who came to life in classic literature that could have been written only by master storytellers like Mark Twain, Rudyard Kipling, and James Baldwin.

As the renowned author of *The Black Stallion*, William Farley, once said: "If you're sincere in your love for horses, you'll manage to have your own someday . . . I envy you the early morning you see your first foal, stilt-legged and wavering, looking at you with large, wondrous eyes while he tries to decide whether you or the mare beside him is his mother."

But until that glorious moment when you become the proud owner of your very own horse, and even if you never do, you'll always be able to think of the horses that you're going to read about here. For they will become as much alive through the written word as any horse you'll ever ride, rope, or tame.

THE PINTO HORSE

(an excerpt from a novel)

by Charles Elliott Perkins

In 1929, after retiring from his glorious career as the president and member of the board of directors of the Chicago, Burlington and Quincy Railroad, CHARLES ELLIOTT PERKINS (1881-1943) moved to Santa Barbara, California, where he bought the Alisal Ranch. Once settled, he filled his property with hearty, powerful horses, one of which, Flying Ebony, became a celebrated winner of the Kentucky Derby.

Because of the experiences he had on his ranch, Perkins was able to write The Pinto Horse *with such realistic detail that in the book's foreword Owen Wister wrote, "It was so true to the cowpuncher West, that no one who had not himself lived that life thoroughly and intimately could possibly have written it; throughout there is nothing made up, faked; nothing transplanted into soil of the sagebrush that in fact grows somewhere else."*

In these captivating first two chapters, Perkins describes the Bull Mountains of Montana, introducing the cowboy Patch Hinton, who has just discovered Pinto, gallant pony born of an English mare and a western stallion. As Pinto grows up, his adventures teach him how to be a successful range horse. Some lessons, however, are more challenging than others. For instance, what will happen when he and his mother are attacked by a ferocious wolf?

Chapter I

In the spring of 1888, "Patch" was running a band of Oregon mares in the Bull Mountains of southern Montana. The Bull Mountains are a range of high and broken hills, sparsely covered with jack pine and heavily grassed in the open parks, with springs at the coulee heads; an ideal winter range for horses. On the south, the country falls away in lessening grassy ridges twenty miles to the Yellowstone. To the north, it drops more steeply to the Mussel Shell Flats.

In those days, the country north of the Yellowstone had not been restocked after the terrible winter of '86, the range was all open to the Canadian line, and the native grass grew in its natural abundance.

From May to November the mares were divided into two bands: one which ranged south to the Yellowstone; the other, to the north of the Bull Mountain hills. Each spring, the Honorable William Spencer Fitzhenry Wantage, third son of the Earl of Palmadime, brought up from his ranch on Powder River the Thoroughbred stallions that were to run with the mares; each November he came for them. In the meantime, all Patch had to do was to ride each morning from his cabin in the foothills, locate his mares, count them, and once a week cross over to the other side of the hills to see that his assistant, Mr. "Slippery Bill" Weston, and the mares that he looked after were in good order. It was a pleasant life; twice a week the Billings stage left the mail in a tin box on the Yellowstone Trail, and once a month Patch hooked up his mule team and drove into Billings for supplies. That trip took three days, and always Patch came back strapped, but happy.

In the autumn, when the stallions had gone back to Powder River, the horses of both bands were brought together to the corrals at the head of Big Coulee, the weanlings branded, the geldings that were to be broken cut out and turned into the saddle-horse pasture, and the balance of the herd turned loose again to winter in the hills.

Range horses know the seasons as well as man, and they know their range as no man ever knows it. They know the pockets where the northers never strike; they know where the warm springs are that never freeze, and they know which ridges are exposed to the Chinooks—warm winds that melt the snow. The range horse loves its native range as no other animal loves its home, and will return to it hundreds of miles, if it has the chance. Especially is this true of mares, which never forget the range where their first foal is dropped. Once a mare has foaled, she will spend the rest of her life within a radius of a few miles, if there is enough feed and water.

The first autumn and winter that Patch had the Oregon mares, he spent all the days and many freezing nights riding to turn them back in their drift toward the west.

When Patch and the Hon. Wm. Spencer Fitzhenry Wantage, who owned a half interest in the horses, were bringing the mares from Oregon, their regular packhorse went lame and they caught what seemed a quiet mare to pack in its place. They haltered the mare and tied her to a tree, packed on her their bedding and cook outfit, and then, as she seemed frightened by the pack sheet, the Honorable, thinking to get her used to it, tied one end to the front of the pack saddle, and, with a corner of the other end in each hand, stood behind her and gave it a flap. The result was electric.

The mare broke away and dashed down the road, the loose sheet flying and flapping above her like a cloud. The first thing she struck was the band of mares, which scattered far and wide; the next thing she ran into was a herd of beef being driven to the railroad; these stampeded like the mares. There were two drummers driving out from town, with a pair, in a top buggy. The flying mare met them head on. The team jack-knifed, broke the pole and a drummer's leg, and disappeared like the beef steers and the mares, while she pursued her unhallowed course into town, wrecked a mounted pageant of the Knights of Columbus, threw the Grand Knight through the plate glass window of the Masonic Hall, and finally fell down herself in the public square.

Patch and the Honorable Wm. Spencer Fitzhenry Wantage spent the next two days rounding up all of the scattered mares that they could find. Twelve they never got, and of these, nine eventually found their way back from Montana to the range in Oregon where they were foaled *eight hundred miles away*, swimming the Snake River to get there.

So Patch was looking after the band of mares on the Bull Mountain range, when one morning in June he rode out to locate them, and to see if Stowaway, the Thoroughbred stallion which had begun his first season on the range a month before, was all right. Over the grassy ridges he jogged, whistling "Garryowen," while the larks, out of sight above, poured down a stream of song. He had found the band the day before and knew, if nothing had disturbed them, he would find them again a few miles farther on toward the Yellowstone. Sure enough, when he was still two miles away, he saw them feeding on a little flat along the cottonwood. But

before he reached them, crossing a dry wash, he came upon
Stowaway, covered with blood and carrying all the marks of
battle, too lame and too sore to climb out of the shallow gully
into which he had staggered.

Patch knew it meant that some range stallion had found
the band, nearly killed Stowaway, and taken them for himself.
That must be seen to. He kicked his pony into a gallop, but
before he had come within one hundred yards of the grazing
mares, a black-and-white spotted stallion came snorting out
to meet him. Indian, thought Patch, escaped from some band
of Crows off their reservation south of the Yellowstone, or
else a wanderer driven from some herd of Crow horses which
had smelled the mares from miles across the river and come
over to get a harem of his own. On came the pinto stallion,
ears back, mouth open, until within twenty yards, Patch
untied his slicker and swung it around his head. The wild
horse slid to a stop, stamped, snorted, and trotted back to
the mares.

It was lucky for him that the cowboy feared Indians
might be camped nearby, or a bullet from his forty-five would
have ended the career of that spotted Don Juan there and
then, for Thoroughbred stallions were scarcer on the
Montana Range than feathered frogs, and Patch was mad; it
would take Stowaway weeks to get over his beating. What
was to be done? He could not shoot the pinto. For though the
Indians were peaceful enough at home, they did not leave
their reservation unless they were up to some mischief; and
in killing a lone cowboy and stealing his horse and guns,
there would be no great risk of discovery in that unsettled
country. There was nothing for it but to start the mares

quietly up the creek toward the corrals, twelve miles away at
the winter camp at the head of Big Coulee; the wild stallion
would go with them, and once started Patch knew that they
would head straight for the corrals where they were regularly
salted. So, with one eye over his shoulder in case of an Indian
surprise, he worked his way to the lower side of the herd,
careful to keep below the rim of the encircling hills.

The Indian stallion dashed to and fro, snorting, always
between Patch and the mares, but the flying slicker kept him
from attacking the saddle horse, and gradually the cowboy
got near enough to turn one grazing mare and then another,
until he had the whole band slowly walking up the creek. For
a mile they strolled on, feeding as they went, and then, as
they got far enough away so that the dust would not be
noticed, Patch crowded the last ones until they began to jog
and then to gallop. After another mile he knew he had them
fully roused, and that they would not stop or turn until they
got to the corrals.

Then Patch pulled up and watched them out of sight—
the wild stallion turning to snort and stamp once more before
he disappeared after the mares. The cowboy loped back down
the creek, and cutting across to where Stowaway was still
standing in the dry wash, dropped his rope over the stallion's
head and started with him to the home camp; but the bat-
tered horse went slowly, and it was mid afternoon when
Patch left him in the shade of some alders half a mile from the
corrals. There, as he hoped, he found the mares, some licking
salt, some rolling in the dust, the pinto stallion just inside the
gate. Patch knew that the only way to get rid of him was to
scare him so badly that he would go back to his own range,

and to do that he would have to catch him. He could not keep the mares in the corral; there was no feed, and if the stallion was not badly scared he would stay in the broken country nearby, and wait until the mares came out. Patch slipped off his horse and crept nearer; the stallion did not wind him, and he got within ten yards, screened by some chokeberry bushes.

Then with a yell he started. The wild horse saw him the fraction of a second too late, and the heavy gate slammed in his face as he reared against it. The rest was simple; the pinto was roped, thrown, and hog-tied, and a lard pail full of stones, the top wired on, tied to his tail. The mares were penned in the second corral, the gate thrown open, the tie-ropes loosed, and the terrified stallion crashed off down the draw, the lard pail banging at his hocks.

That night, thirty miles to the south, the sleeping Indians on the Little Horn clutched each other in terror, and their frightened ponies scattered to the hills.

Chapter II

One May morning, when Patch was counting the mares, a year after he had tied the lard pail to the painted stallion, he missed Bald Stockings, a Thoroughbred English mare that the Honorable Wantage had turned on the range with Stowaway. Patch did not try to find her, but a week later as he went to get his saddle horse in the morning, he found her in the corral licking salt, and beside her a wobbly-legged pinto foal. Bald Stockings snorted and trotted to the far end of the corral as Patch shut the gate. For half an hour he could not get near her, but he knew horses; so for the first few minutes he sat on the fence and whistled, and gradually as the mare quieted he strolled nearer, until he could rub her nose and then her neck; then he left her and went about his day's work.

Late that afternoon he tried again, and this time with little trouble he haltered her, and soon the foal, too, would allow him to scratch its back. For a week Patch kept the mare in the hay corral, and by that time the foal would follow him about and lick his hand for sugar. The pinto colt started life with confidence in man, and Patch knew that someday that confidence would save him much trouble. Later, the mare joined the band, and each day when Patch counted them he gave the foal some sugar. Before the end of the summer it would leave the band and trot to meet him when he whistled the first few bars of "The Spanish Cavalier."

Bald Stockings was a good mother; the colt grew fast, and as the summer drifted by he learned the lessons of the range: how to stick close to his mother's side, so as not to be stepped on or knocked down when the band of mares was galloping; how to give Stowaway a wide berth; how to keep one eye always on the watch for prairie dog holes; and also about wolves—that was a terrifying experience. One hot noon, Pinto lay stretched out asleep on a hillside; Bald Stockings gradually had grazed on fifty yards down the swale. The foal never knew exactly what happened. There was a snarling rush which knocked him over as he scrambled to his feet. He heard his mother squeal, and the next thing he knew she was striking and biting at a gray thing that writhed on the grass, while another gray streak vanished over the ridge. It was over in a minute, and the mare, with nostrils flaring and a red light in her great wild eyes, was nuzzling the still dazed foal. The gray thing on the grass was still; but before they trotted off to join the band the big mare shook it like a rag, while the foal huddled against her. And ever afterward, when he smelt the wolf smell, he remembered; and when he was older, he would follow it to kill, sometimes with success, until no wolf of that range would come near any band of horses that Pinto ran with.

September came and went; the long strings of wild geese went honking overhead, and the quaking aspen had yellowed in the gulches, when one morning two men strange to Pinto helped Patch drive the band of horses to the big corrals. There Pinto was whistled from the band, and there was much talk that he did not understand. Then he and Bald Stockings were driven into a smaller corral where they waited, snorting, while the dust went up in clouds in the main corral, and the smell of burning flesh and hair added terror to the shouts of men, the wild calls of the mares, and the squeals of branded foals. Pinto did not know until long after that Patch had bought the Hon. Wantage's half interest in him, and had declared that he should never be disfigured with a brand.

Late that afternoon, with the first winter storm breaking overhead, when the band of mares was turned out and driven into the foothills to their winter range, Bald Stockings and Pinto were turned into the saddle-horse pasture with the geldings, and there Pinto spent his first winter, feeding on the buffalo grass when the Chinooks swept the ridges clear, warm and snug in the hay corral when a wild norther roared down from the Canadas. And always he kept learning; for every few days Patch whistled him from the others to give him a bite of sugar or a piece of bread, so that he never had the range horse's fear of man.

From the wise old geldings he learned to find the least windy spots along the wind-swept hillsides; he learned how to paw through the crust and get the sweet grass underneath, when the strongest bull would have starved, for no member of the cow family has learned to break the crust with its feet, and so when it cannot push through the snow with its nose, it dies, where a range horse fattens. He learned something too of the tactics of war; for the veteran geldings would fight like wolves for a warm pocket in which to feed, or a specially sheltered nook near the haystacks, on the bitter winter nights when the sky over the Mussel Shell shivered with the Northern Lights. Once there was an attack of wolves, but the geldings, without excitement, almost with indifference, headed in a circle, in the center of which were Bald Stockings and Pinto, presenting an unbroken battery of heels, which only one rash wolf dared venture, only to be hurled back, a broken thing, and torn to pieces by his ravening friends. Bald Stockings was for breaking out into open attack, but the sour old geldings knew better and met her with flattened ears and clicking teeth, and the wolves, half fed on their foolish companion, slunk away.

THE GREAT WOODEN HORSE

as retold by James Baldwin

Born in Indiana within a Quaker colony, JAMES BALDWIN *(1841-1925) was the author of over fifty books. Because of the isolating atmosphere in which he grew up, Baldwin was mostly self-educated, but he still managed to write or edit more than half of the school texts used in the United States at that time.*

In fact, despite his lack of formal education, Baldwin, at the age of twenty-four, went on to become a teacher, and later a superintendent of Indiana grade schools for eighteen years. Well respected among his peers, he then received an honorary doctorate degree in philosophy from DePauw University, and his books were read in schools as far away from his native America as China, Japan, and the Philippine Islands.

When did Baldwin begin to cherish books? According to his mother, Baldwin "was not born with a silver spoon under his tongue, but with a book in his hand. When other babies would cry for their bottles, he would cry for books."

In his Wonder-Book of Horses, from which the following selection was taken, Baldwin recounts the famous Greek myth about the gigantic wooden horse left within the walls of Troy by its enemies, the Greeks, led by one of the most famous and clever Grecian soldiers, Ulysses. What was inside this colossal wooden horse? Read on . . .

I. The Puzzled Trojans

Of all the wooden horses that men have ever made, he was the hugest. Yet he was not very handsome. Built hastily of rough-hewn maple planks and of beams and spars from the wrecks of unseaworthy ships, the great wonder is that he was so well made. But old Epeus, who planned and directed the building of the huge fellow, was a master carpenter, the most skillful in the world; and the rough pieces of timber were fitted together with such nicety that there was no crack, nor crevice, nor point of weakness, in any part of the work. Certain men who were jealous of Epeus's fame whispered that it was not he but the goddess Athena who did it all; and this we shall not deny.

Early one morning the people of Troy were astonished to learn that the Greeks, who had been besieging their city for ten weary years, had sailed away during the night. Nobody had seen them go, nobody knew whither they had gone; but anybody, by climbing up to the watchtower above the Scæan gate, could see that they had utterly vanished. The sandy beach where a thousand ships had been drawn up was deserted and bare, save that it was strewn with the ruins of the huts and tents that had so long sheltered the persistent Greeks. A short distance to the left, and half concealed behind a growth of tall reeds, was a dark object which puzzled the Trojan watchmen not a little. When first seen in the gray light of dawn, it looked like some huge sea monster, black and slimy, just emerged from the water.

"Great Neptune is with us!" cried one of the men. "He has sent a creature out of the deep, and it has swallowed up our enemies and their tents and their ships, and left not one to tell the tale."

"Nonsense!" said another, who had sharper eyes. "This thing looks to me like no creature at all, but rather a statue of some kind which the Greeks have built, and left behind them as a token of their disappointment and defeat. And now I remember that I have seen crowds of them busy at work on the same spot for several days. I have no doubt but that they are all far over the sea by this time, and this east wind will waft them swiftly to their own country."

All Troy, when it awoke and heard the glad news, stretched itself out and took a long breath. The shopkeepers threw open their doors and hung up their handsomest goods where they would catch the eyes of the passers-by. The farmers brought out their plows and mended their old harnesses and talked about the big crops they would raise in the fields that had lain fallow so long and had been enriched with so much human blood. The housewives returned to their long-neglected spinning, or overhauled their linen closets, and brushed the cobwebs out of their bedchambers. The citizen-soldiers hung up their bows and quivers, their swords and shields, and each began to furbish up the instruments of his trade. The maidens donned their best gowns and went out to walk and smile sweetly. The small boys with their fishing lines in their pockets, and the great crowd of idlers who always expected to grow rich upon what they could find, hastened into the streets and elbowed their way to the gates, only to find them closed.

About noon, however, the gate next to the sea was thrown wide open. A great multitude poured out, and the mad race that was made for the shore was like the scramble of boomers on our western frontier when lands are given away by the government. Soon thousands were on the beach, looking eagerly for whatever the Greeks might have dropped, but seldom finding anything more valuable than a broken comb, a bit of leather, or some small pieces of crockery. All were shy of the southern part of the beach, where the strange monster stood among the reeds. Everybody could plainly see now that it was a horse. Its huge head, its arching neck, its broad back, its flowing tail were visible from every part of the beach; and the boys who had ventured nearest said that it stood firmly on a broad platform of planks.

That it was an immense horse, and that it was made of wood, nobody could dispute. But why had the Greeks built it, and why had they left it there? Presently a number of the king's counselors came out to look at the strange object and decide what to do with it. Some advised that it should be drawn into the city and lodged within the tower, there to be a kind of permanent exposition of the folly of the Greeks. Others were in favor of throwing it into the sea, or of kindling a fire beneath it and burning it to ashes.

The dispute would doubtless have ended in blows had not Laocoön, a prince of Troy and priest of Apollo, come hastily out from the city with a small company of soldiers.

"What folly is this?" he cried. "Who wants to take anything into the city that the Greeks have left upon our shores? As for my part, I would look with dread upon any gift that they might offer us. This horse is not so harmless as he looks. Either there are men within his giant body, or he is so put together that when he is taken into the city he will fly into pieces, knock down our walls, and destroy our houses. Throw him into the sea, burn him to ashes, do anything but receive him within our walls."

Having said this, he hurled his heavy spear at the monster. The weapon struck it full in the breast, where it remained quivering, and those who stood nearest fancied that they heard deep, hollow groans issuing from the throat of the beast.

"To the sea with him! To the sea with him!" cried a hundred voices.

"What a fine blaze he will make!" cried others. And they ran hither and thither gathering sticks and driftwood with which to kindle a fire beneath him.

II. The Captured Greek

In great danger then was the sturdy beast, and the Trojans would have made an end of him right quickly had not something happened to change their minds. Suddenly a great hubbub was heard some distance down the beach, and men and boys, forgetting the horse for the moment, ran hurriedly to the spot to see what was going on. A party of peasants were dragging toward the city a young man who, covered with mud and blood, and with his hands tied behind him, seemed a target for every kind of insult. His clothing told that he was a Greek.

"Hold on!" cried one of the king's counselors. "Bring the fellow here, and stop your noise. We will see what he can tell us about his friends and this strange monster that they have left on our shores. Who are you, wretch, and where are your people who so lately were encamped on this very spot?"

"My name," said the captive, "is Sinon, and I am by birth a Greek. But people I have none; for the Greeks have condemned me to death, and now ye Trojans also seek my life. Where, indeed, shall I turn when kinsmen and foes would alike slay me?"

These words, spoken in sweet and persuasive tones, touched the hearts of the rude rabble, and they paused to hear what further the young man would say.

"Speak on," said the king's counselor, "and tell us by what cruel fate you have been left behind by your countrymen to fall into the hands of your foes."

"It is a long story," responded to the young man, "but I will not weary you. For more than a year the crafty Ulysses has been plotting my destruction, for no other reason than because I once befriended a chief whom he dislikes. When, at length, three months ago the Greeks decided in council to give up this war and return to their own land, he saw his opportunity. Storms swept across the sea, and the south wind brought tempests in its train, and the ships dared not leave their moorings. Then the chiefs called together the soothsayers and asked them what should be done to appease the gods, that so they might have favorable winds and a smooth sea for their home-returning voyage. And one of them, Eurypylus, declared that nothing short of a human sacrifice would turn aside the vengeful ire of Apollo; the other, Calchas, explained that since the Greeks had stolen the statue of Athena which stood in your great temple of Troy, that goddess would never suffer them to return to their native land until they had reared on these shores the massive figure of a horse to be a witness to their repentance. Then the chiefs asked who should be the victim to be offered up to Apollo, and Calchas, urged on by Ulysses, answered, "Sinon." Forthwith, I was bound with cords, fillets were tied about my temples, and the knife was sharpened, ready to pierce my heart. But on the night before the rueful day, I burst my bonds and escaped to the slimy marshes, where I lay hidden until I saw my countrymen embark and sail away in their thousand ships across the sea to distant Greece. Then, almost dead from hunger and privation, I ventured out, only to be seized by these rude peasants and dragged to this place as you see me now."

"But the horse—the horse!" cried the Trojans. "What about the horse?"

"I have already told you," answered Sinon, "that the image was built to appease the wrath of the goddess Athena. The soothsayers declared that not only would it bless its builders, but that into whatever city it should go, there it would carry good fortune and peace and prosperity. The Greeks, however, were unwilling that it should bring happiness to you, their foes, and hence they built it very large, and so tall that it could not pass through any of your gates; and they placed it here close to the reedy marsh, in the hope that, when the autumn rains fell and the sea raged furiously, the waves would beat upon and overwhelm it and carry it away, and no people whatever should be blessed by its presence."

"Ah! That is their game, is it?" cried the Trojans with one voice. "Well, we'll see about that. We'll have the good horse inside our walls this very night."

Then there was great shouting and rejoicing on every side, and those who had been the first to wreak their spite upon Sinon were the first to undo his bonds and wipe the blood from his face, and find food for him to eat. Forthwith two companies of men were sent to the city, one to bring long, strong ropes, and the other to make a breach in the wall large enough to allow the great horse to be drawn through.

III. The Fate of Laocoön

In the meanwhile a fearful tragedy was being enacted on the beach. Laocoön, the priest of Apollo, had built an altar on the sands and was making ready to offer up a sacrifice, as had been the custom of his country from ancient times. His two sons stood beside him, one on either hand, ready to do their part. Suddenly loud shouts arose from those who were near-est the sea, and everybody fled in dismay. Looking out toward the island of Tenedos, Laocoön saw two huge serpents swim-ming with wondrous speed toward the land. He smiled at the cowardly fears of the people, and would not desert the altar which he had raised. He doubtless thought that the reptiles were mere water snakes, and that they would not venture upon the land. But in this he was sadly mistaken, for upon reaching the beach the serpents reared their heads high in the air and glided with the swiftness of light over the sands. Ere Laocoön and his boys could make a single movement toward escape, the horrid creatures had reached the altar; they had twined their slimy folds around the necks and limbs of three unfortunates; they had crushed them to death in their terrible embrace. The people who saw this awful tragedy from a dis-tance were spellbound with horror, nor did they know who might be the next victim. But the serpents, when they had done their deadly work, glided quietly away and hid themselves beneath an altar which the Greeks had erected to Athena.

"Behold the vengeance of the goddess!" cried some of the people.

"She has punished Laocoön for his wickedness in smiting the great horse with his spear!" cried others.

"Such be the fate of all who would try to thwart the will of the ever-living powers!" cried the priests. Let us hasten to appease Athena by drawing her horse into the city and giving it the shelter which it ought to have."

IV. The Success of the Stratagems

By this time, the men who had been sent after ropes had returned; bringing also stout wheels to be placed underneath the platform whereon the horse stood. With infinite trouble a slip-knot was thrown over the huge wooden head, and long ropes were attached to each of the four legs. Then, with the aid of levers and pulleys, the whole huge mass was lifted a little at a time, and the smooth-sliding wheels were fastened in their places, one under each corner of the platform. This being done, as many as could get near enough seized hold of the ropes, the word of command was given, and the three long lines of tugging men and boys moved slowly over the plain, dragging the horse behind them. When they drew near the city the whole populace came out to meet them, and the glad shouts which rent the air seemed louder than the cries which warriors utter on the field of battle.

A wide breach had been opened in the wall, and through this, just as the sun was dipping into the sea, the horse was

pushed into the city. Once, when the huge body struck against a projecting stone, the Trojans who were nearest were astonished to hear the rattling of shields, and some turned pale and looked around with dread, and forgot to join in the chorus of song that was raised in welcome to the image that was to bring peace and good fortune to Troy. Soon darkness came, and the tired people hastened to their homes. Not a soldier remained to guard the broken wall, not a watchman stayed at his post above the gates. Worn out with the excite- ment of the day, everybody retired early to rest.

About midnight a man crept stealthily along the dark streets, and came finally to the breach that had been made in the wall. With a little lantern and a kettle of pitch in one hand, he climbed up the rough stones to the top. Once there, he sat down for a moment and gazed steadily toward the sea. The moon, now just rising behind him, lighted up the great expanse of water, and he could plainly see not only the long line of beach with the waves rippling upon the sand, but the dark outline of Tenedos Island lying in the shadows four miles farther away. But what did he see between the island and the shore? A thousand ships with their dark hulls just visible above the water, and all propelled by twenty thousand oars that glinted strangely in the moonlight as they rose and fell. The Greeks, who had lain hidden all day behind Tenedos, were returning to the Trojan shore—in a few min- utes their vessels would be drawn up in their old places along the white beach.

The man on the wall seemed greatly pleased with what he saw. Rising again to his feet, he hung the kettle of pitch by a chain upon the outside of the wall, and into it he dropped a bit of blazing pine which he had lighted with his lantern. Soon a lurid flame arose from the burning mass. It lighted up the plain and was reflected upon the top of the wall, showing the face of the man. It was Sinon, the young Greek.

Immediately answering lights appeared on the ships, and Sinon clambered hastily to the ground. The huge figure of the wooden horse loomed up in the moonlight before him. With the flat of his sword he struck each of its legs three times. Then suddenly there was a great sound of rattling armor above him. The creature seemed to be strangely endowed with life. In a moment there was a noise as of the shooting of bolts and the grating of hinges; a narrow door was opened in the horse's breast, and a gleaming helmet, with a man's face beneath it, was thrust out.

"Is that you, Sinon?"

"It is I, Ulysses."

"Is all well?"

"All is well. The ships are already drawn up upon the sands. The Greeks are marching across the plain. The witless Trojans are asleep and dream not of danger."

Then a rope was let down from the open door, and Ulysses, fully armed, slid hand over hand to the ground. Other heroes followed, all encased in armor, and all right glad to escape from their prison house.

"The trick has succeeded even better than any of us hoped," said Ulysses. "And now for the last act in this long and weary war! Let fire and sword do their work!"

I need not tell you how the gates were thrown open to the Greeks, nor how the Trojans were awakened from their dreams of peace only to meet death at the hands of their foes, nor how the torches were applied to palace and hut and the whole city was wrapped in flames. The horse had nothing to do with all this. Amid the smoke and fire, and the din of rattling arms and the shouts of the victors, he stood all the rest of the night and through the morning hours. Toward noon, however, Ulysses and Sinon, passing by the spot, observed that he had disappeared. Whether in the confusion Athena had claimed him and carried him away, or whether he had been mysteriously endowed with life and had galloped out of the burning city to find refuge in the woods and mountains, neither of these heroes could tell.

BARNACLES

Who Mutinied for a Good Cause

by Sewell Ford

Born in South Levant, Maine, SEWELL FORD settled in Haverhill, Massachusetts, at the age of fourteen, and shortly after high school graduation became a reporter for The Haverhill Gazette. *Although he didn't begin writing fiction until his mid-thirties, Ford did enjoy a twenty-year span of successful literary publication and is credited with contributing several hundred short stories to magazines and newspaper syndicates across the country.*

Among his extensive works are a number of delightful horse stories, including "Barnacles," about a patient old horse bought by a salty sea captain in order to please his bride-to-be. Unfortunately, the couple seem mismatched from the start, for the captain knows little else but the sea, and his fiancée wants nothing to do with boats. Imagine the hilarious results when the captain tries to appease her needs and his own by putting wheels on his boat and letting Barnacles pull it. Well, let's just say the captain's idea makes a real splash!

With his coming to Sculpin Point there was begun for Barnacles the most surprising period of a more or less career which had been filled with unusual equine activities.

For Barnacles was a horse, a white horse of unguessed breed and uncertain age.

Most likely it was not, but it may have been Barnacles's first intimate connection with an affair of the heart. Said affair was between Captain Bastabol Bean, owner and occupant of Sculpin Point, and Mrs. Stashia Buckett, the unlamenting relict of the late Hosea Buckett.

Mrs. Buckett it was who induced Captain Bastabol Bean to purchase a horse. Captain Bean, you will understand, had just won the affections of the plump Mrs. Buckett. Also he had, with a sailor's ignorance of feminine ways, presumed to settle offhand the details of the coming nuptials.

"I'll sail over in the dory Monday afternoon," said he, "and take you back with me to Sculpin Point. You can have your dunnage sent over later by team. In the evenin' we'll have a shore chaplain come 'round an' make the splice."

"Cap'n Bean," replied the rotund Stashia, "we won't do any of them things, not one."

"Wha-a-at!" gasped the Captain.

"Have you ever been married, Cap'n Bean?"

"N-n-no, my dear."

"Well, I have, and I guess I know how it ought to be done. You'll have the minister come here, and you'll come to marry me. You won't come in no dory, either. Catch me puttin' my two hundred an' thirty pounds into a little boat like that. You'll drive over here with a horse, like a respectable person, and you'll drive back with me, by land and past Sarepta Tucker's house so's she can see."

Now for more than thirty years Bastabol Bean, as master of coasting schooners up and down the Atlantic seaboard,

had given orders. He had taken none, except the formal directions of owners. He did not propose to begin taking them
now, not even from such an altogether charming person as
Stashia Buckett. This much he said. Then he added:

"Stashia, I give in about coming here to marry you; that
seems no more than fair. But I'll come in a dory and you'll go
back in a dory."

"Then you needn't come at all, Cap'n Bastabol Bean."

Argue and plead as he might, this was her ultimatum.

"But Stashia, I ain't got a horse, never owned one an'
never handled one, and you know it," urged the Captain.

"Then it's high time you had a horse and knew how to
drive him. Besides, if I go to Sculpin Point I shall want to
come to the village once in a while. I sha'n't sail and I sha'n't
walk. If I can't ride like a lady, I don't go to the Point."

The inevitable happened. Captain Bean promised to buy a
horse the next day. Hence his visit to Jed Holden and his intro-
duction to Barnacles, as the Captain immediately named him.

As one who inspects unfamiliar objects, Captain Bean
looked dazedly at Barnacles. At the same time Barnacles
inspected the Captain. With head lowered to knee level, with
ears cocked forward, nostrils sniffing and underlip twitching
almost as if he meant to laugh, Barnacles eyed his prospective
owner. In common with most intelligent horses, he had an
almost human way of expressing curiosity.

Captain Bean squirmed under the gaze of Barnacles's big,
calm eyes for a moment, and then shifted his position.

"What in time does he want, anyway, Jed?" demanded
the Captain.

"Wants to git acquainted, that's all, Cap'n. Mighty

knowin' hoss, he is. Now some hosses don't take notice of anything. They're just naturally dumb. Then again you'll find hosses that seem to know every blamed word you say. Them's the kind of hosses that's wuth havin'."

"S'pose he knows all the ropes, Jed?"

"I should say he did, Cap'n. If there's anything that hoss ain't done in his day, I don't know what 'tis. Near's I can find out, he's tried every kind of work, in or out of traces, that you could think of."

"Sho!" The Captain was now looking at the horse in an interested manner.

"Yes, sir, that's a remarkable hoss," continued the now enthusiastic Mr. Holden. "He's been in the cavalry service, for he knows the bugle calls like a book. He's traveled with a circus—ain't no more afraid of elephants than I be. He's run on a fire engine—know that 'cause he wants to chase old Reliance every time she turns out. He's been a streetcar hoss, too. You jest ring a door gong behind him twice an' see how quick he'll dig in his toes. The feller I got him off'n said he knew of his havin' been used on a milk wagon, a peddler's cart, and a hack. Fact is, he's an all-around worker."

"Must be some old by your tell," suggested the Captain. "Sure his timbers are all sound?"

"Dun'no 'bout his timbers, Cap'n, but as fer wind an' limb you won't find a sounder hoss, of his age, in this county. Course, I'm not sellin' him fer a four-year-old. But for your work, joggin' from the Point into the village an' back once or twice a week, I sh'd say he was jest the ticket; an' forty-five, harness an' all as he stands, is dirt cheap."

Again Captain Bean tried to look critically at the white

horse, but once more he met that calm, curious gaze and the attempt was hardly a success. However, the Captain squinted solemnly over Barnacles's withers and remarked:

"Yes, he has got some good lines, as you say, though you wouldn't hardly call him clipper built. Not much sheer for'ard an' a little too much aft, eh?"

At this criticism Jed snorted mirthfully.

"Oh, I s'pose he's all right," quickly added the Captain. "Fact is, I ain't never paid much attention to horses, bein' on the water so much. You're sure he'll mind his helm, Jed?"

"Oh, he'll go where you point him."

"Won't drag anchor, will he?"

"Stand all day if you'll let him."

"Well, Jed, I'm ready to sign articles, I guess."

It was about noon that a stable-boy delivered Barnacles at Sculpin Point. His arrival caused Lank Peters to suspend peeling the potatoes for dinner and demand explanation.

"Who's the hoss for, Cap'n?" asked Lank.

It was a question that Captain Bean had been dreading for two hours. When he had given up coasting, bought the strip of Massachusetts seashore known as Sculpin Point, built a comfortable cottage on it, and settled down within sight and sound of the saltwater, he had brought with him Lank Peters, who for a dozen years had presided over the galley in the Captain's ship.

More than a mere sea-cook was Lank Peters to Captain Bean. He was confidential friend, advising philosopher, and mate of Sculpin Point. Yet from Lank had the Captain carefully concealed all knowledge of his affair with the Widow Buckett. The time of confession was at hand.

In his own way, and with a directness peculiar to all his acts, did Captain Bean admit the full sum of his rashness, adding thoughtfully: "I s'pose you won't have to do much cookin' after Stashia comes; but you'll still be mate, Lank, and there'll be plenty to keep you busy on the Point."

Quietly and with no show of emotion, as befitted a sea-cook and a philosopher, Melankthlon Peters heard these revelations. If he had his prejudices as to the wisdom or folly of marrying widows, he said no word. But in the matter of Barnacles he felt more free to express something of his uneasiness.

"I didn't ship for no hostler, Cap'n, an' I guess I'll make a poor fist at it, but I'll do my best," he said.

"Guess we'll manage him between us, Lank," cheerfully responded the Captain. "I ain't got much use for horses myself; but as I said, Stashia, she's down on boats."

"Kinder set in her ideas, ain't she, Cap'n?" insinuated Lank.

"Well, kinder," the Captain admitted.

Lank permitted himself to chuckle guardedly. Captain Bastabol Bean, as an innumerable number of sailor-men had learned, was a person who generally had his own way. Intuitively the Captain understood that Lank had guessed of his surrender. A grim smile was barely suggested by the wrinkles about his mouth and eyes.

"Lank," he said, "the Widow Buckett an' me had some little argument over this horse business an'—an'—I give in. She told me flat that she wouldn't come to the Point if I tried to fetch her by water in the dory. Well, I want Stashia mighty bad; for she's a fine woman, as you'll say when you know her. So I promised to bring her home by land and with a horse. I'm bound to do it, too. But by time!" Here the Captain suddenly slapped his knee. "I've just been struck with a notion. Lank, I'm going to see what you think of it."

For an hour Captain and mate sat in the sun, smoked their pipes, and talked earnestly. Then they separated. Lank began a close study of Barnacles's complicated rigging. The Captain tramped off toward the village.

Late in the afternoon the Captain returned riding in a sidebar buggy with a man. Behind the buggy they towed a skeleton lumber wagon—four wheels connected by an extension pole. The man drove away in the sidebar, leaving the Captain and the lumber wagon.

Barnacles, who had been moored to a kedge anchor, watched the next day's proceedings with interest. He saw the Captain and Lank drag up from the beach the twenty-foot dory and hoist it up between the wheels. Through the forward part of the keelson they bored a hole for the kingbolt. With nut-bolts they fastened the stern to the rear axle, adding some very seamanlike lashings to stay the boat in place. As finishing touches they painted the upper strakes of the dory white, giving to the lower part and to the running gear of the cart a coat of sea green.

Barnacles was experienced, but a vehicle such as this amphibious product of Sculpin Point he had never before seen. With ears pointed and nostrils palpitating from curiosity, he was led up to the boat-bodied wagon. Reluctantly he backed under the raised shafts. The practice-hitch was enlivened by a monologue on the part of Captain Bean, which ran something like this:

"Now, Lank, pass aft that backstay (the trace) and belay; no, not there! Belay to that little yardarm (whiffletree). Got it through the lazy-jack (trace-bearer)? Now reeve your jib-sheets (lines) through them deadeyes (hame rings), and pass 'em aft. Now where in Tophet does this thingumbob (holdback) go? Give it a turn around the port bowsprit (shaft). There, guess everything's taut."

The Captain stood off to take an admiring glance at the turnout.

"She's down by the bow some, Lank, but I guess she'll lighten when we get aboard. See what you think."

Lank's inspection caused him to meditate and scratch his head. Finally he gave his verdict: "From midships aft she looks as trim as a liner, but from midships for'ard she looks scousy, like a Norwegian tramp after a voyage 'round the Horn."

"Color of old Barnacles don't suit, eh? No, it don't, that's so. But I couldn't find no green-an'-white horse, Lank."

"Couldn't we paint him up a little, Cap'n?"

"By Sancho, I never thought of that!" exclaimed Captain Bean. "Course we can; git a string an' we'll strike a waterline on him."

With no more ado than as if the thing was quite usual, the preparations for carrying out this indignity were begun. Perhaps the victim thought it a new kind of grooming, for he made no protest. Half an hour later old Barnacles, from about the middle of his barrel down to his shoes, was painted a beautiful seagreen. Like some resplendent marine monster shone the lower half of him. It may have been a trifle bizarre, but with the sun on the fresh paint, the effect was unmistakably striking. Besides, his color now matched that of the dory's with startling exactness.

"That's what I call real ship-shape," declared Captain

Bean, viewing the result. "Got any more notions, Lank?"

"Strikes me we ought to ship a mast so's we could rig a spritsail in case the old horse should give out, Cap'n."

"We'll do it, Lank; fust-rate idea!"

So a mast and spritsail were rigged in the dory. Also the lines were lengthened with rope, that the Captain might steer from the stern sheets.

"She's as fine a land-goin' craft as ever I've seen anywhere," said the Captain, which was certainly no extravagant statement.

How Captain Bean and his mate steered the equipage from Sculpin Point to the village, how they were cheered and hooted along the route, how they ran into the yard of the Metropolitan Livery Stable as a port of refuge, how the Captain escaped to the home of Widow Buckett, how the "splicin'" was accomplished—these are details which must be slighted.

The climax came when the newly made Mrs. Bastabol Buckett Bean, her plump hand resting affectionately on the sleeve of the Captain's best blue broadcloth coat, said cooingly: "Now, Cap'n, I'm ready to drive to Sculpin Point."

"All right, Stashia, Lank's waitin' for us at the front door with his craft."

At first sight of the boat on wheels Mrs. Bean could do no more than attempt, by means of indistinct ejaculation, to express her obvious emotion. She noted the grinning crowd of villagers, Sarepta Tucker among them. She saw the white and green dory with its mast, and with Lank, villainously smiling, at the top of a step-ladder which had been leaned against the boat; she saw the green wheels, and the verdant gorgeousness of Barnacles's lower half. For a moment she gazed at the fantastic equipage and spoke not. Then she slammed the front door with an indignant bang, marched back into the sitting room and threw herself on the haircloth sofa with an abandon that carried away half a dozen springs.

For the first hour she reiterated, between vast sobs, that Captain Bean was a soulless wretch, that she would never set foot on Sculpin Point, and that she would die there on the sofa rather than ride in such an outlandish rig.

Many a time had Captain Bean weathered Hatteras in a southeaster, but never had he met such a storm of feminine fury as this. However, he stood by like a man, putting in soothing words of explanation and endearment whenever a lull gave opportunity.

Toward evening the storm spent itself. The disturbed Stashia became somewhat calm. Eventually she laughed hysterically at the Captain's arguments, and in the end she compromised. Not by day would she enter the dory wagon, but late in the evening she would swallow her pride and go, just to please the Captain.

Thus it was that soon after ten o'clock, when the village folks had laughed their fill and gone away, the new Mrs. Bean climbed the stepladder, bestowed herself unhandily on the midship thwart, and with Lank on the lookout in the bow and Captain Bean handling the reins from the stern sheets, the honeymoon chariot got under way.

By the time they reached the Shell Road, the gait of the dejected Barnacles had dwindled to a deliberate walk which all of Lank's urgings could not hasten. It was a soft July night with a brisk offshore breeze, and the moon had come up out of the sea to silver the highway and lay a strip of milk-white carpet over the waves.

"Ahoy there, Lank!" shouted the bridegroom. "Can't we do better'n this? Ain't hardly got steerageway on her."

"Can't budge him, Cap'n. Hadn't we better shake out the spritsail? Wind's fair abeam."

"Yes, shake it out, Lank."

Mrs. Bean's feeble protest was unheeded. As the night wind caught the sail and rounded it out, the flapping caused old Barnacles to cast an investigating glance behind him. One look at the terrible white thing which loomed menacingly above him was enough. He decided to bolt. Bolt he did to the best of his ability, all obstacles being considered. A down-grade in the Shell Road, where it dipped toward the shore, helped things along. Barnacles tightened the traces, the sprit-sail did its share, and in an amazingly short time the odd vehicle was spinning toward Sculpin Point at a ten-knot gait. Desperately Mrs. Bean gripped the gunwale and lustily she screamed:

"Whoa, whoa! Stop him, Captain, stop him! He'll smash us all to pieces!"

"Set right still, Stashia, an' trim ship. I've got the helm," responded the Captain, who had set his jaws and was tugging at the rope lines.

"Breakers ahead, sir!" shouted Lank at this juncture.

Sure enough, not fifty yards ahead, the Shell Road turned sharply away from the edge of the beach to make a detour by which Sculpin Point was cut off.

"I see 'em, Lank."

"Think we can come about, Cap'n?" asked Lank, anxiously.

"Ain't goin' to try, Lank. I'm layin' a straight course for home. Stand by to bail."

How they could possibly escape capsizing Lank could not understand, until just as Barnacles was about to make the turn he saw the Captain tighten the right-hand rein until it was as taut as a weather-stay. Of necessity Barnacles made no turn, and there was no upset. Something equally exciting happened, though.

Leaving the road with a speed he had not equaled since the days when he had figured in the Grand Hippodrome Races, his seagreen legs quickened by the impetus of the affair behind him, Barnacles cleared the narrow strip of beach grass at a jump. Another leap and he was hock-deep in the surf. Still another, and he split a roller with his white nose.

With a dull chug, a resonant thump, and an impetuous splash, the dory entered its accustomed element, lifting some three gallons of saltwater neatly over the bows. Lank ducked. The unsuspecting Stashia did not, and the flying brine struck fairly under her ample chin.

"Ug-g-g-gh! Oh! Oh! H-h-h-elp!" spluttered the startled bride, and tried to get on her feet.

"Sit down!" roared Captain Bean. Vehemently Stashia sat.

"W-w-w-we'll all b-b-be d-d-drowned, drowned!" she wailed.

"Not much we won't, Stashia. We're all right now, and we ain't goin' to have our necks broke by no fool horse, either. Trim in the sheet, Lank, an' then take that bailin' scoop." The Captain was now calmly confident and thoroughly at home.

Drenched, cowed, and trembling, the newly made Mrs.

Bean clung despairingly to the thwart, fully as terrified as the plunging Barnacles, who struck out wildly with his green legs, and snorted every time a wave hit him. But the lines held up his head and kept his nose pointing straight for the little beach on Sculpin Point, perhaps a quarter of a mile distant.

Somewhat heavy weather the deep-laden dory made of it, and in spite of Lank's vigorous bailing the water sloshed around Mrs. Bean's boot-tops, yet in time the sail and Barnacles brought them safely home.

"'Twa'n't exactly the kind of honeymoon trip I'd planned, Stashia," commented the Captain, as he and Lank steadied the bride's dripping bulk down the stepladder, "and we did do some sailin', in spite of ourselves; but we had a horse in front an' wheels under us all the way, just as I promised."

Danny and Broncho

(an excerpt from a novel)

by Richard Ball

Born in Reynoldstown, Ireland, in 1897, RICHARD BALL has had little written about him except that he went to Clongowes Wood College, the same school that the famous Irish author James Joyce attended. Said to love hunting and steeplechasing, Ball, who published Danny and Broncho *in 1930, was also the author of* The Better Part, Hounds Will Meet, Penny Farthing, *and* Young Jack Fellowes.

In keeping with the tradition of the horse as man's heroic and courageous companion through battle and adventure, Danny and Broncho *extends the legend of the gallant horse. From the valiant Bucephalus, who saved Alexander the Great in battle, to the fearless black Arabian Broiefort, who rescued the Dane Ogier from the fierce Moors, Broncho represents this century's champion.*

Set in World War I, the novel tells of how Broncho accompanies his beloved owner, Roger Arbuthnot, to battle. After bravely fighting in France, the wounded Roger is separated from Broncho, who, while long-ing for his faithful friend, eventually adapts to his new setting on a farm. In this excerpt, Chapter 15, we see Broncho arriving on the farm and first meeting a redheaded youth named Danny Keogh, who later will grow to love the fine-spirited war-horse as much as Broncho's former companion in battle ever did.

Chapter XV

Hands in his pockets, tattered cap on the back of his head, Danny Keogh, Billy Foley's "boy of work," came whistling into the yard one February morning.

"Hi!" called a voice behind his back.

"Sir?" he answered, springing round.

"There's a horse to come off the half-nine train," ordered Bill. "You'll go meet him when you get your work done."

"Right, sir!" answered Danny. "What's he—a ridin' horse? Will I want to bring you a bridle?"

"I dunno," said Bill. "He's a horse that's comin' over from me brother Larry."

Danny nodded wisely. He hoped it would be a "ridin'" horse. There'd been nothing in the place these many months, and he'd been lonesome for a hunt! And so, in good time, he set off briskly along the road to the town.

Undersized, freckled-faced, red-haired, Danny fed the pigs and chopped the wood and did all the odd jobs about the farm; but his heart was given to the horses—even such as came and went through Bill's hands. And now, since Bill himself had got too heavy, he had been promoted to the position of stable "jock," and so he hoped very ardently that the new horse would be something he could ride about.

Still whistling, he eventually arrived at the station. "Got a horse waitin' for me, Jack?" he inquired from the porter.

The latter, sitting on the booking-office windowsill, nodded slowly.

"There's something beyond in the box."

"Come along then, me son," said Danny. "I've got no

48

time to spare."

Jack the porter roused himself.

"Shut up your chat, Danny Keogh," he advised.

But Danny dodged from the cuff that accompanied the advice, and set off whistling down the platform. He scrambled into the box, and stretched out a grimy hand to the dark object that stood shivering in its depths.

Softly he spoke to the stranger.

"What's ailin' you? You needn't be a-feard of me. Come here, me son, and let me put the bridle on you . . ." Then, through the half-open door to Jack the porter: "Faith, this old skin's half dead of fright!"

At last the bridle was on. At last the porter let down the door. At last Broncho blundered out into the sunlight, and Danny could take stock of his charge. All at once his heart gave a bound.

"A grand horse!" he announced. "A grand horse! But he's afraid of his mortal life. Look, Jack, I can scarcely get me hand on him!"

Yet he did. Shivering violently, at last Broncho allowed that grimy paw to stroke his shoulder.

Danny glanced around in triumph, but there was no praise forthcoming from Jack the porter.

"Take himself and yourself out of this," the latter advised, "and don't be cutting up all the station yard."

∞

Bill Foley's fifty acres stretched upward across the hillside, and about midway up the white thatched farmhouse stood, facing southward across the sloping valley toward the mountains. As Broncho walked slowly into the farmyard he glanced about him with a dull apprehension. But though there was much which seemed strange, there was nothing to prove alarming. On the contrary, all the farmyard inhabitants seemed contented to a degree. The fowls scarcely troubled to move from beneath his tired feet. And a sow and her family, searching the manure heap methodically, never even looked up.

At the farmhouse door Danny halted, raising his tattered cap to run his fingers through his shock of red hair.

"Are you there, Mrs. Foley?" he shouted. "Is himself within?"

In answer, a tall woman emerged, the fowls hurrying across the yard to meet her as she appeared at the door.

"No, he isn't," she answered slowly. "He's away up the hill." And then, with an increase of interest, she added: "And so that's the horse from England?"

"That's him," Danny agreed.

"The creature!" she exclaimed. "You can see every bone in his body! Can't you put him in the stable now and come in till I give your dinner? Himself can see him when he comes down."

"So he can," assented Danny. He took another quick glance at his charge. "He's no bad cut of a horse either, Mrs. Foley. Jack, below at the station, was sayin' he was grand."

Mrs. Foley paused on her way back toward the house.

"Grand, how are you!" she said, glancing round again. "Sure, they're all grand until something goes wrong with them. Only you mightn't tell himself that!"

Danny laughed lightly, giving a jerk to the reins.

"Come along, me son," he said, turning to Broncho. And as he slipped the bridle off a moment later in the darkness of the stable he added, with a final friendly pat on the horse's shoulder: "You needn't be a-feard of me. You and me'll have to get friends!" Then he hastily made his way in to his dinner.

But he was no more than halfway through a huge mouthful of potato before heavy footsteps on the cobblestones of the yard told him that "himself" was coming in.

"Bad luck to it!" he said with a grimace, glancing at the clock on the kitchen dresser. "He'll scarcely give me time to swallow a bit before he has me out again paradin' out the horse!"

Such proved the case.

"Well, did you get him?" was Bill Foley's first question.

"Yes, sir," answered Danny, his mouth very full.

"And you're not long back?"

"Only come this minute!"

"I suppose you spent the whole mornin' gallivantin' down at the station? Hurry up now and come out an' put a rope on him till I see him. What sort of horse is he, anyway?"

"Ah! Grand, sir," answered Danny. "He's grand."

Bill turned away with the heavy footsteps of later middle age. About that, he thought, he'd have to decide for himself! But sometimes, he admitted, he didn't do too badly with the horses that came over from Larry. If they weren't sound enough to make a price for him, they sometimes won a few pounds!

Slowly he made his way out again. In appearance he was a stouter and shorter edition of his brother, despite the complete absence of the obvious "horsiness"—the pepper-and-salt breeches, the low-crowned bowler hat—which made part of Larry's stock-in-trade. But he had the same small, cute blue eye, that "eye for a horse" which was hereditary in them both. And it came to rest approvingly, that afternoon, upon Broncho.

"Grand cut of an old horse," Bill mused slowly. "Quality! Best I saw comin' here this long time." Slowly he bent down and ran his hand along Broncho's tendons. "But them legs could do with a bit of a rest. I'll clasp a bit of a blister on him an' let him out down below on the bog."

He straightened his back again and adjusted his greasy hat onto to his forehead.

"Bring me the can of gas tar," he ordered Danny.

He held the halter in one hand, noting with a shrewd eye Broncho's lackluster gaze and weary expression, while Danny hurried across the yard and came back again with the can.

"Now," he ordered, "dip in your hand, and clap it on his legs."

Danny dipped. Breathing earnestly, he smeared Broncho's legs heavily from the knee down to the fetlock. Then he paused, glancing back questioningly at his employer.

"Will that do, sir?"

Bill nodded.

"Well enough. Clean your hands, an' catch a-hold of him."

A moment later Danny came back again.

"Will I put him back in the stable, sir?" he questioned, taking hold of the rope.

"You will not," answered Bill with slow emphasis.

"What then—?" The boy stood irresolute, the halter rope swinging loose from his hand.

"Oh, bring him down to the bog, can't you, and let him out with the others."

"What, now, sir?" protested Danny. "An' he only after comin' off the train!"

"Yes, now," said Bill shortly. "Do you think there's time here to spend doctorin' him? And when you come back, don't be long about goin' up to pick the stones off the new grass field."

Danny went—very slowly, Broncho dragging along wearily behind. In the big field down by the river that was known as the bog, he finally slipped the halter off the old horse's head.

"Well, take care of yourself now," he whispered affection-ately. "If you want your fill here you'll have to warm yourself lookin' for it. But I'll bring you down a handful of something whenever I get the chance." And Broncho, looking back at him, almost seemed as if he understood.

Very slowly Danny walked up again to the yard. In imagi-nation he had seen himself spend that spring perched upon Broncho's back, riding about the roads to the envy of his fel-lows, but instead it would seem that his immediate task was to be many dreary days stone-picking in the new grass field!

"An' I hoped," he confided to Mrs. Foley that evening as he drank his tea, "that come the first of May I'd be ridin' him below at the races."

"Races, how are you?" answered Mrs. Foley with asper-ity. "It would answer you better if you saw about keeping the sow out of the garden!"

But Bill's treatment, drastic though it may have seemed, served Broncho in good stead. Abrupt though the change had been, the keen winds of spring revived his failing vitality. The turfy bog pasture was soft to his tired feet. The short, sweet grass that came with spring gave tone to his worn system. March passed. April gave place to May. A greenness came upon the countryside. The hedges burst forth into leaf. The hawthorn blossomed white. From the woods came the cuckoo's mocking call. In the reeds by the riverside the water-fowl hatched out their young. And down in the long narrow field that ran along by the river, Broncho continued to grow strong, spending the sunny days in a lazy luxuriance, in company with the old gray mare, and the two-year-old that had been fired, and the chestnut horse with the curly hocks.

Very often Danny stole down to see him, and his ragged pocket never failed to hold a few handfuls of oats. And so, gradually, amid the peace and quiet of the summertime country-side—so different from the noisy routine of the East Range lines, where all Captain Willoughby's care had gone unrequited!—those dark memories of the past began once more to fade. Less and less often did those old terrors come back to trouble him, and as he grew stronger he was more able to shake them off when they did. And gradually, too, amid the quiet of those fields, which were so like those in which long ago he had been foaled and reared, there was borne upon him the realization that once more he had a friend. He came to listen for Danny's blithe whistle behind the hedge, to prick his ears in greeting as the quick footsteps came toward him in the grass. And as their friendship grew, often in the cool of the summer evenings as Danny crouched by the riverbank, watching the trout nibble at his line, from behind his back would come the sound of Broncho's quiet

footsteps and the next moment the horse's nose would come sniffing at his pockets. And since to Danny Broncho now meant more than all the trout that lurked in the pools, rod and line would be abandoned until he had had his talk with the horse.

What talks those were! What daydreams were woven of the day when together they would "come trottin' home at the point-to-point!" And Broncho, gazing with wise eyes at the freckled face beneath the ragged cap, felt that for Danny he would do a great deal. His old strength had returned. The long months of rest, the peaceful surroundings, the lush luxuriance of the summer's grass had one and all played their parts—as had Bill Foley's blistering to his joints and tendons! Danny, running his thin fingers down the horse's legs, used to murmur his hopes beneath his breath. "Clean as a whistle," he assured himself. "Faith, there isn't so much as a mark on one of them! Stand work, is it? Faith, they'd stand all the work in the world!" And jerking his red forelock back off his forehead again, he would look up at Broncho with admiring eyes. "Aye, bags of it, old son!" he would murmur, stroking the horse's muzzle with grimy hand.

One afternoon toward the end of August, Bill himself came down to the bog. He had often come before, upon his general round of the farm. But this time there seemed to be a new purposefulness about his steady stride, a new expression in his shrewd blue eye. He came straight across the field to where Broncho was grazing. The horse, hearing the heavy footsteps approach, looked up at him with questioning gaze.

Bill looked him over long and carefully, noted the strong, clean legs from which the blister had peeled away, noted the returned confidence with which he once again held up his head.

"He ought to stand now," he said to himself. "I'll try him for a month or two, anyway."

He walked slowly 'round, looking at the horse from every angle. Broncho's summer coat completely hid his old shrap-nel scars.

"Begad," mused Bill, "you wouldn't know he was the same horse. That's where the oats was going, I'll go bail!" But maybe he thought it would be no harm! The horse looked like having a chance in him. Anyway, he'd let Danny knock him about for a bit. . . . The young lad wouldn't ask any bet-ter, and he was a good sort of young lad if he was kept in his place! Not but that—all the summer—he hadn't been able to get any satisfaction out of him as to what had been happening to the oats!

A Horse's Tale

(an excerpt from a short story)

by Mark Twain

*Born in Missouri to John Marshall and Jane Lampton Clemens,
Samuel Langhorne Clemens, better known as* MARK TWAIN *(1835-
1910), is most remembered for his colorful stories about life on the
Mississippi River described in such famous novels as* The Adventures
of Huckleberry Finn *and* The Adventures of Tom Sawyer. *When
his father died in 1847, Twain, then eleven, supported his family by
taking on odd jobs ranging from that of a grocery clerk to a blacksmith's
assistant. It was in these early years, however, that the renowned author
first began to write and display his wit and humor. Then, at the early
age of seventeen, his hard work paid off with his first publication, "The
Dandy Frightening the Squatter," which appeared in* Carpet-Bag, *a
Boston newspaper.*

*Set on adventure, the young Twain later traveled west to Nevada
and California. It was there, after hearing a strange story about a jumping frog, that the soon-to-be-famous Missourian wrote the short story
that would launch his writing career, "The Celebrated Jumping Frog of
Calaveras County." From that moment on, the popular writer was
nicknamed the "Washoe Giant" and the "Wild Humorist of the Sage
Brush Hills."*

*Finally successful, Twain married Olivia Langdon, and the couple
later had three daughters. But because of his reckless economic ventures,*

Twain and his family soon became financially ruined. Calling on the enterprising nature of his youth, Twain began to lecture worldwide, especially in England, and finally, with this money coming in and with the help of his friend Henry Hulleston, who led him toward some sound stock investments, Twain was once again financially stable.

But as much as popularity pursued Twain, so did tragedy. His daughter Susy suddenly died in 1895 at the tender age of seven, and his wife, who herself was in poor health and trying to recover in Italy, died eight years later, in 1903. The grief-stricken Twain, who had been at her bedside, returned to the United States, bought a home in Connecticut, and set to work on his autobiography.

Not known for writing about horses, but using them often in much of his work, Twain incorporated one of his best writing techniques— using everyday language that nearly all readers could relate to—when he wrote "The Horse's Tale." Told from the horse's point of view, this clever story tells the tale of Buffalo Bill's horse, Soldier Boy, "born of Kentucky blood and bronco spirit," who listened to the gossip of the humans and animals at Fort Paxton and then delightfully retold it in this charming narrative.

Part I

Soldier Boy—Privately to Himself

I am Buffalo Bill's horse. I have spent my life under his saddle—with him in it, too, and he is good for two hundred pounds, without his clothes; and there is no telling how much he does weigh when he is out on the war-path and has his batteries belted on. He is over six feet, is young, hasn't an

ounce of waste flesh, is straight, graceful, springy in his motions, quick as a cat, and has a handsome face, and black hair dangling down on his shoulders, and is beautiful to look at; and nobody is braver than he is, and nobody is stronger, except myself. Yes, a person that doubts that he is fine to see should see him in his beaded buckskins, on my back and his rifle peeping above his shoulder, chasing a hostile trail, with me going like the wind and his hair streaming out behind from the shelter of his broad slouch. Yes, he is a sight to look at then—and I'm part of it myself.

I am his favorite horse, out of dozens. Big as he is, I have carried him eighty-one miles between nightfall and sunrise on the scout; and I am good for fifty, day in and day out, and all the time. I am not large, but I am built on a business basis. I have carried him thousands and thousands of miles on scout duty for the army, and there's not a gorge, nor a pass, nor a valley, nor a fort, nor a trading post, nor a buffalo-range in the whole sweep of the Rocky Mountains and the Great Plains that we don't know as well as we know the bugle calls. He is Chief of Scouts to the Army of the Frontier, and it makes us very important. In such a position as I hold in the military service, one needs to be of good family and possess an education much above the common to be worthy of the place. I am the best educated horse outside of the hippodrome, everybody says, and the best-mannered. It may be so, it is not for me to say; modesty is the best policy, I think. Buffalo Bill taught me most of what I know, my mother taught me much, and I taught myself the rest. Lay a row of moccasins before me—Pawnee, Sioux, Shoshone, Cheyenne, Blackfoot, and as many other tribes as you please—and I can name the tribe every moccasin belongs to by the make of it. Name it in horse-talk, and I could do it in American if I had speech.

I know some of the Indian signs—the signs they make with their hands, and by signal-fires at night and columns of smoke by day. Buffalo Bill taught me how to drag wounded soldiers out of the line of fire with my teeth; and I've done it, too; at least I've dragged him out of battle when he was wounded. And not just once, but twice. Yes, I know a lot of things. I remember forms and gaits and faces, and you can't disguise a person that's done me kindness so that I won't know him thereafter wherever I find him. I know the art of searching for a trail all by myself, with Buffalo Bill asleep in the saddle; ask him—he will tell you so. Many a time, when he has ridden all night, he has said to me at dawn, "Take the watch, Boy; if the trail freshens, call me." Then he goes to sleep. He knows he can trust me, because I have a reputation. A scout horse that has a reputation does not play with it.

My mother was all American—no alkali-spider about her, I can tell you; she was of the best blood of Kentucky, the bluest Blue-grass aristocracy, very proud and acrimonious— or maybe it is ceremonious. I don't know which it is. But it is no matter; size is the main thing about a word, and that one's up to standard. She spent her military life as colonel of the Tenth Dragoons, and saw a deal of rough service—distin-guished service it was, too. I mean, she carried the Colonel; but it's all the same. Where would he be without his horse? He wouldn't arrive. It takes two to make a colonel of dra-goons. She was a fine dragoon horse, but never got above that. She was strong enough for the scout service, and had the endurance, too, but she couldn't quite come up to the

63

speed required; a scout horse has to have steel in his muscle and lightning in his blood.

My father was a bronco. Nothing as to lineage—that is, nothing as to recent lineage—but plenty good enough when you go a good way back. When Professor Marsh was out here hunting bones for the chapel of Yale University, he found skeletons of horses no bigger than a fox bedded in the rocks, and he said they were ancestors of my father. My mother heard him say it; and he said those skeletons were two million years old, which astonished her, and made her Kentucky pretensions look small and pretty antiphonal, not to say oblique. Let me see . . . I used to know the meaning of those words, but . . . well, it was years ago, and 'tisn't as vivid now as it was when they were fresh.

That sort of words doesn't keep, in the kind of climate we have out here. Professor Marsh said those skeletons were fossils. So that makes me part bluegrass and part fossil; if there is any older or better stock, you will have to look for it among the Four Hundred, I reckon. I am satisfied with it. And am a happy horse, too, though born out of wedlock.

And now we are back at Fort Paxton once more, after a forty-day scout, away up as far as the Big Horn. Everything quiet. Crows and Blackfeet squabbling—as usual—but no outbreaks, and settlers feeling fairly easy.

The Seventh Cavalry still in garrison, here; also the Ninth Dragoons, two artillery companies, and some infantry. All glad to see me, including General Alison, commandant. The officers' ladies and children as well, called upon me— with sugar. Colonel Drake, Seventh Cavalry, said some pleasant things; Mrs. Drake was very complimentary; also

Captain and Mrs. Marsh, Company B, Seventh Cavalry; also the Chaplain, who is always kind and pleasant to me, because I kicked the lungs out of a trader once. It was Tommy Drake and Fanny Marsh that furnished the sugar—nice children, the nicest at the post, I think.

That poor orphan child is on her way from France—everybody is full of the subject. Her father was General Alison's brother; married a beautiful young Spanish lady ten years ago, and has never been in America since. They lived in Spain a year or two, then went to France. Both died some months ago. This little girl that is coming is the only child. General Alison is glad to have her. He has never seen her. He is a very nice old bachelor, but is an old bachelor just the same and isn't more than a year this side of retirement by age limit; and so what does he know about taking care of a little maid nine years old? If I could have her it would be another matter, for I know about children, and they adore me. Buffalo Bill will tell you so himself.

I have some of this news from overhearing the garrison gossip; the rest of it I got from Potter, the General's dog. Potter is a Great Dane. He is privileged, all over the post, like Shekels, the Seventh Cavalry's dog, and visits everybody's quarters and picks up everything that is going in the way of news. Potter has no imagination, and no great deal of culture, perhaps, but he has a historical mind and a good memory, and so he is the person I depend on mainly to post me up when I get back from a scout. That is, if Shekels is out on depredation and I can't get hold of him.

THE HORSE OF GENGHIS KHAN

Mysterious Mongolia Leaves Its Imprint in the Life of a Parisian Traveler

by Paul Morand

PAUL MORAND *(1888-1976), considered to be one of France's most imaginative and accomplished writers, intrigues readers with daring and absorbing adventures of distant lands. As the son of the gifted artist Eugène Morand, Paul grew up in Paris surrounded by such famous artists as actress Sarah Bernhardt, dramatist Oscar Wilde, and sculptor Auguste Rodin.*

After World War I, Morand served as a diplomat in various embassies in London, Madrid, and Rome. His experiences lent a cosmopolitan air to his writing, and gave it a flair for adventure.

As it was in his childhood, Morand found himself in the constant company of artists when he was an adult. Among his companions were the famous authors Jean Giraudoux and Marcel Proust; the talented film director of an early version of Beauty and the Beast, *Jean Cocteau; and the immortal poet Ezra Pound. Undoubtedly influenced by the creative and inspiring atmosphere he lived in, Morand produced more than sixty works of poetry, fiction, and memoirs.*

In "The Horse of Genghis Khan," the reader meets eccentric young wanderer Erik La Bonn, who while traveling with a caravan across the Gobi Desert discovers an unusual horse's skull that changes not only his luck, but that of everyone who dares to own it!

Erik La Bonn crossed the Great Wall of China at P'ing Fu and headed in the direction of Leng K'on Pass. Mongolia lay unfolded before him, flat as a board into which, twisting like a corkscrew, the little caravan was entering. This caravan was made up of horses, mules, two blue carts drawn by mules, carriers, teamsters, and the traveler himself. Erik La Bonn was an eccentric young wanderer, as independent as his long nose proclaimed him to be, and passionately devoted to the open road. He was on his way from Peking back to Europe on horseback, for he was much less afraid of perishing from the cold than suffocating in the heat of the Trans-Siberian Railroad coaches. For days he had thus been on the march, all alone, singing Parsifal to himself at the top of his lungs, his long legs dangling from the flanks of the Mongolian pony; and since his was not a costume such as one might think to be worn on a trip like this, but a city-cut overcoat, tight at the waist, long trousers, a starched, stand-up collar, and a gray derby hat (which he wore on principle) he caused a great deal of astonishment among the Chinese he met, and, of course, was taken for a very high personage.

The caravan crossed rivers which proved great obstacles, being so sinuous that they had to be forded as often as fifteen times. Finally, they entered the Gobi Desert. They met Bactrian camels, whose thickening fur already heralded the approaching winter; soldiers on furlough, without pay, and who had eyes like wolves'; merchants sitting in their traps, accompanied by their wives, placidly drawing puffs of smoke through their water pipes; missionaries of the Foreign Bible Society, sharpers who displayed great dexterity in the shell game at which the Mongolians stand ready to lose their souls and their dollars.

One evening, being a little bored with these sights, which were always the same, Erik La Bonn had pushed ahead of his escort to visit a hunting pavilion, halfway up a hill which had been built for the great emperor Kien Lung. He lost his way and found that he was alone in a desolate valley strewn with stones and boulders. For days, to be sure, there had not been any trees, but never until this moment had he felt the vast and naked grandeur of Asia. Even the beaten path had disappeared: It seemed that after several smaller paths had become entangled with it and spread it out in several different directions, the path had stopped of its own accord on the edge of a void—on the very brink of an underworld.

La Bonn did not know what fear was. He carried no weapons on his travels except mustard, with which, as he used to say, he defended himself during the day against the vile taste of the native cooking, and he sprinkled it on his bed at night to keep the vermin away. He had been told that bandits only held the rich Nomad families for ransom and hardly ever molested Europeans, so that he really dreaded nothing but the tenacity of the beggars and the smell of the Mongolian women. He stopped: around him nothing but debris of porphyrus rock, shafts of abandoned coal mines, and a blinding sun which set the dry autumn air on fire. Suddenly, some twenty or thirty yards away, he noticed a striking object on the ground; at first he took it to be a mirror. He went up to it and found it to be the skull of a horse. There was no sign of a skeleton. This skull was so white, so highly polished by many winds and rains, so perfect in substance, so strangely shaped, with its sloping indentation of a nose, and the empty,

horrible-looking hollows of the eyes—so religious almost in its stripped barrenness, that it seemed to date from the very first years of the existence of this earth.

Erik La Bonn alighted from his horse and took the object in his hands; it was terribly heavy. For a long time this modern Hamlet, having placed the skull on his knees, lost himself in thoughts. Were these the last remains of some caravan, which, overtaken by the fierce, salty winds, had perished there of thirst? Was this the last vestige of the moment of some departed Mongolian prince, in a red robe, repulsive and goitrous, a standard bearer or clan chieftain perhaps, sent to guard one of the outer bastions of the Great Wall? Or perhaps the sole surviving witness of some great battle fallen here, cornered by the wolves? A horse! La Bonn thought of the days of Sung, when the horse was king, celebrated by all the poets, immortalized by the best artists, and to be found, either in clay effigies or in its natural state, in every tomb. The horse, without which none of the great migrations could have taken place! This immense, stony valley was only deserted now because its former inhabitants, the Mongols, the Huns, and the Turks, had been able, thanks to their horses, to gain and conquer China, India, and Europe. Genghis Khan had been the master of the world then, but the master of Genghis Khan's world was his horse.

Softness of the skin is a sign of youth, but the polish on the skeleton is proof of its great age. From the horse's skull, which had taken on the lustre of ivory, the flesh had, no doubt, dropped centuries ago. La Bonn let his imagination run riot, and, exalted by his solitude and the luminous cloud of such grand relics, he lost sense of time and space and fell asleep. He dreamed that he had found the head of Genghis Khan's horse and that he could never part with it again.

He was at last torn out of his dream by the arrival of his escort which joined him just about as night was falling and which he found prostrated on the ground as he awakened. The sight of that skull filled those men with a holy terror. He had his precious find lifted into the cart, and the march was resumed. The howls of wild dogs could already be heard; the smell of goatskins and smoke, carried over to them by the wind, proclaimed that a village was near. And in fact, a long wall of dried mud was outlined against the horizon, punctuated by dim lights. They were approaching Jehol, "The Town of Complete Virtue."

He had to stop at a fourth-rate hotel—one of the kind that are called pork-taverns in China—because it was market day and all the other hostelries were filled. Goatskins were drying in the open air; their smell hardly obscured the stench of manure and sewage which ran openly down the middle of the only street. Pelts from Dzingary were being lifted onto the backs of camels by great big devils in blue tunics; a Chinese checker in yellow coat and hat traced characters in Chinese ink on the reverse sides, directing the pieces to a port on the Pacific Ocean, en route to America.

The servants prepared the bed in the guest room. La Bonn was waiting for his dinner to be cooked, which consisted of millet cakes. He had affixed the horse's skull outside of his room; it was soon surrounded by a crowd of curious people who contemplated it awestruck and with fright. Women with flat and otherwise deformed feet came to have a look at it; beggars' dogs with a scowling expression, their hair standing on end, and yellow lamas with shaven heads remained to mill about the strange fetish of the white man.

It was plain that the indifferent and skeptical Chinese had been left far behind, that one was in the midst of those superstitious and wild Mongolians, son of a country particularly given to magic and all sorts of devilish practices. Soon the crowd became so large that the courtyard of the inn was completely filled. The pork bladders, which served as lamps, were lighted. At just about that time the clandestine opium vendors and the managers of the Jehol theater sent a delegation to make a complaint that the resorts of pleasure were empty and to request that the stranger go to his room and kindly remain there.

The next day, after having left his calling card at the governor's—leaving one's calling card is regarded in the Orient as a propitious rite and is a rigid requirement of good form—Erik La Bonn went to the temple. This was another monument of dried mud, of no definite epoch, located outside the town in the midst of a dirt and refuse dump. There Buddha smiled. La Bonn was received by a priest who was half doctor, half sorcerer, clad in yellow silk; quite a pleasant person. In the usual roundabout fashion La Bonn put several questions to him. He had him asked if in these parts any particular faith or belief was attached to animal bones, more specially a horse's skull. The answer that he received was that every kind of skeleton was a dangerous abomination, because the greedy souls of a body are always hovering about it in order to reincarnate themselves. A horse's skull had often enriched its finder, but caused his male progeny to perish. Women pregnant more than five months should stand in fear of it. However, everything depended on the day on which the object had been found.

Last night . . . ?

That was one of the very worst days, said the lama. One of the most dreaded on the whole calendar. Although prayers might yet be said before nightfall, still there was little hope. There was really nothing else to do but to fly before the invisible, to fool the demons, or to burn the skull. La Bonn shrugged his shoulders at all this nonsense and gave orders to have his find attached to his saddle. And from them on the horse's skull never left that place.

Thus he traveled through central Asia. An invisible protection seemed to emanate from the skull: Bandits never came near the caravan; nowhere was hospitality refused. La Bonn was allowed to wash in the sacred hot springs, and when he reached the country of the great pastures he had always had his share of fresh meat, and almost every night he found a wooden bed under those strange tents of the nomadic Mongolians, quarters made of such thick felt that they were as hot inside as one of those Norwegian cookers in which food can be boiled without fire. When he met lamas, bent on pilgrimages to Tibet, they honored him by offering him tea. Every evening La Bonn hung the skull outside of his tent on a pole driven into the ground.

The reception was not only cordial in Mongolia, but was equally friendly in Turkestan, in Kokand, and Bukhara. The religions, the customs, and the color of the skins changed, but the horse's skull continued to receive the respect of everyone. The population, becoming gradually Moslem, welcomed La Bonn as no European had been received since the arrival of the Bolsheviks. Even the customs inspectors let him pass duty-free.

One evening La Bonn arrived at the Gare de l'Est in Paris with the skull of Genghis Khan's horse under his arm. Sentimental effusions, accompanied by verbose lyricism, gushed from him whenever he talked about it. However, he spoke of it seldom, for those people who were slaves of petty habits, jostled about in narrow streets, boxed up in ugly, tall houses, have not the least understanding for the beauties of the steppes and the life of the nomad. La Bonn could not find an apartment and so had to content himself with a small hotel room in the Quartier Latin. In it there was a Louis Philippe bed—much too large—and a mirrored cabinet, so that he could hardly open his wardrobe trunks. First he put the skull under the dressing table, then on the mantelpiece. This relic, as majestic and provoking as it had been when he found it back there in the Gobi Desert, had become nothing more than a piece of refuse from a butcher shop, in Paris, a skeleton for a ragpicker; the dust had made a shabby object of it, turned it a gray color. But La Bonn did not have the nerve to get rid of it, nor even confess that its possession embarrassed him considerably.

An Englishwoman, Lady Cynthia D., heard about the horse of Genghis Khan and became exceedingly interested in the subject. As a matter of fact, she was only interested in the young Frenchman, but she begged La Bonn to entrust to her that which remained of the Mongolian courser; she said that she would hang the skull over her bed. Through the eyes of the skull she put blue ribbons which came out by the nostrils, thus robbing the dramatic relic of its last mystery. La

Bonn had to restrain her from gilding it. Two days after she had hung the horse's head over her bed, Lady Cynthia was lying down when a great noise was heard in her room. People entered and found her bathed in her blood. The cursed thing had detached itself from the wall and had split the head of the young Englishwoman in two. She only recovered after a great amount of suffering. She did not want to hear any more of the horse's head nor of its owner, and after this accident the horse of Genghis Khan went back to Quartier Latin.

La Bonn kept it for some time, but on the eve of a journey entrusted it to a retired deep-sea captain, who was an invalid. This simple man—although grown more imaginative since he had been compelled to lead a sedentary life—had waxed enthusiastic over La Bonn's mule and had asked for the privilege of keeping the skull during the absence of his friend. The much-traveled La Bonn then began to receive strange letters from the captain which became disquieting, and finally totally demented. He was just preparing to return when he learned that the old mariner had been found one morning suspended from the window fastening. On the table, in plain view, was the horse's head. La Bonn hoped that the captain's heirs would inherit it and took pains not to give a sign of life. But on the very next day after his return, he received a call from a notary who informed him that he had been made the captain's sole heir, and that the skull would be returned to him so soon as the seals had been broken. Then these things happened: A little later La Bonn gave it to a painter for a still life, but the latter's studio burned down. He gave it to a raffle, but the number that should have won it was never presented. People began to know the history of the skull. The servants did not dare enter the room anymore on account of the "haunted head," as they called it. It seemed indeed that all the mishaps which the heavens had spared La Bonn and which, without dropping, had remained suspended over his head, and the strange immunity which he enjoyed, were suddenly interrupted as soon as the skull left his hands. He did not dare destroy it for fear of some curse befalling him. He could no longer risk giving it away for fear of participating in a crime.

"Alas! You, the last remains of the companion of the greatest conqueror the world has ever known," thought La Bonn, "perhaps there is nothing you fear more than rest. Perhaps you are anxious to escape from among these sedentary lives where I have put you, to regain your freedom? And is that the reason why you perpetrate these crimes? Perhaps what you like in me is a taste similar to your own for a life which is a continuous journey, a passion for moving on to always new countries, and climates which are never the same?"

It was night, and La Bonn, thus soliloquizing, looked from his bed at the horse's skull, which the light of the moon was illuminating with a soft silver glow which had nothing earthly in it and seemed to resemble the color of infinite space.

La Bonn knew the moment had come. It would be now or never. He put an overcoat on over his pajamas, took the skull on his shoulders, and went down to the street; it weighed a great deal. Soon it was necessary to carry it in both hands. Finally La Bonn reached the bridge de l'Alma. A cold wind was blowing, which reminded him of the great winds of the steppes. The Seine curved gently as it flowed past the

Trocadero, the two towers of which were outlined against the sky, darker than the night. After ceasing to be royal a little farther up, as it passed in front of the Louvre, the Seine now abandoned itself to romantic gracefulness as it flowed on to Passy. Erik La Bonn placed the skull on the railing of the bridge. He was thinking of the great Siberian streams, of the torrents of the Chinese river Altai, of the Mongolian tributaries swallowed up by the salty and thirsty sand. . . . How small the Seine was, how shallow for such an adventure—such an end! But is there ever an end to anything?

The electric lights lit up the river and gave it a rose color, like those face lotions they sell in beauty parlors. . . . La Bonn thrust the skull out into the black void. . . . There was a silence. Then a splash. Evidently its great weight would make it sink straight to the bottom. . . . But no . . . a miracle! The skull floated! Yes, that heavy object actually floated, carried along by the current like a piece of paper. La Bonn saw distinctly how it took the middle of the stream, then gently sheered off to the left, following the bend of the river.

Genghis Khan's horse, that gem of the Mongolian steppes, had started out again. Where would it go? Perhaps it would be stopped tomorrow by some obstacle, by a fisherman, by the hands of a child. Or perhaps, free to gain the open sea, it would become a strange seahorse. Would it ride about the dungeons of the sea, with the taste of salt—the same taste as that of the great Mongolian desert, which still clings to the memory that it was once a sea?

BLUE BLAZES
And the Marring of Him
by Sewell Ford

Formerly a prominent journalist for New York, Baltimore, and Boston newspapers, SEWELL FORD (1866-1946) traded his newspaper career to write fiction in 1901. His literary fame came with his widely acclaimed "Torchy and Shorty McCabe" stories, the former of which were made into a series of films.

The author of over ten works of fiction, many of which were about horses, this prolific writer took a different turn with "Blue Blazes," taken from his collection of horse stories, Horses Nine.

Typically described as beautiful, courageous steeds with sweeping manes and glossy coats, horses throughout literature are most unlike the "unhandsome colt" that Ford describes here in this story. A true misfit, this defiant horse develops a friendship that withstands both time and distance with a runaway boy who is as much of a misfit as Blue Blazes himself.

Those who should know say that a colt may have no worse luck than to be foaled on a wet Friday. On a most amazingly wet Friday—rain above, slush below, and a March snorter roaring between—such was the natal day of Blue Blazes.

And an unhandsome colt he was. His broomstick legs seemed twice the proper length, and so thin you would hardly have believed they could ever carry him. His head, which somehow suggested the lines of a bootjack, was set awkwardly on an ewed neck.

For this pitiful, ungainly little figure only two in all the world had any feeling other than contempt. One of these, of course, was old Kate, the sorrel mare who mothered him. She gazed at him with sad old eyes blinded by that maternal love common to all species, sighed with a huge content as he nuzzled for his breakfast, and believed him to be the finest colt that ever saw a stable. The other was Lafe, the chore boy, who, when Farmer Perkins had stirred that little fellow roughly with his boot-toe as he expressed his deep dissatisfaction, made reparation by gently stroking the baby colt and bringing an old horse blanket to wrap him in. Old Kate understood. Lafe read gratitude in the big, sorrowful mother eyes.

Months later, when the colt had learned to balance himself on the spindly legs, the old sorrel led him proudly about the pasture, showing him tufts of sweet new spring grass and taking him to the brook, where were tender and juicy cowslips, finely suited to milk teeth.

In time the slender legs thickened, the chest deepened, the barrel filled out, the head became less ungainly. As if to make up for these improvements, the colt's markings began to set. They took the shapes of a saddle-stripe, three white stockings, and an irregular white blaze covering one side of his face and patching an eye. On chest and belly the mother sorrel came out rather sharply, but on the rest of him was that peculiar blending which gives the blue roan shade, a color unpleasing to the critical eye and one that lowers the market value.

Lafe, however, found the colt good to look upon. But Lafe himself had no heritage of beauty. He had not even grown up to his own long, thin legs. Possibly no boy ever had hair of such a homely red. Certainly few could have been found with bigger freckles. But it was his eyes which accented the plainness of his features. You know the color of a ripe gooseberry, that indefinable faint purplish tint; well, that was it.

If Lafe found no fault with Blue Blazes, the colt found no fault with Lafe. At first the colt would sniff suspiciously at him from under the shelter of the old sorrel's neck, but in time he came to regard Lafe without fear, and to suffer a hand on his flank or the chore boy's arm over his shoulder. So between them was established a gentle confidence beautiful to see.

Fortunate it would have been had Lafe been master of horses on the Perkins farm. But he was not. Firstly, there are no such officials on Michigan peach farms; secondly, Lafe would not have filled the position had such existed. Lafe, you see, did not really belong. He was an interloper, a waif who had drifted in from nowhere in particular, and who, because of a willingness to do a man's work for no wages at all, was allowed a place at table and a bunk over the wagon shed. Farmer Perkins, more jealous of his reputation for shrewdness than of his soul's salvation, would point to Lafe and say, knowingly: "He's a bad one, that boy is; look at them eyes." And surely, if Lafe's soul-windows mirrored the color of his mental state, he was indeed in a bad way.

In like manner, Farmer Perkins judged old Kate's unhandsome colt.

"Look at them ears," he said, really looking at the unsightly nose-blaze. "We'll have a circus when it comes to breakin' that critter."

Sure enough, it was more or less of a circus. Perhaps the colt was at fault, perhaps he was not. Olsen, a sullen-faced Swede farm-hand whose youth had been spent in a North Sea herring boat, and whose disposition had been matured by sundry second mates on tramp steamers, was the appropriate person selected for introducing Blue Blazes to the uses of a halter.

Judging all humans by the standard established by the mild-mannered Lafe, the colt allowed himself to be caught after small effort. But when the son of old Kate first felt a halter he threw up his head in alarm. Abruptly and violently his head was jerked down. Blue Blazes was surprised, hurt, angered. Something was bearing hard on his nose; there was something about his throat that choked.

Had he, then, been deceived? Here he was, wickedly and maliciously trapped. He jerked and slatted his head some more. This made matters worse. He was cuffed and choked. Next he tried rearing. His head was pulled savagely down, and at this point Olsen began beating him with the slack of the halter rope.

Ah, now Blue Blazes understood! They got your head and neck into an arrangement of straps and rope that they might beat you. Wild with fear, he plunged desperately to right and left. Blindly he reared, pawing the air. Just as one of his hoofs struck Olsen's arm, a buckle broke. The colt felt the nose-strap slide off. He was free.

A marvelous tale of fierce encounter with a devil-possessed colt did Olsen carry back to the farmhouse. In

proof he showed a broken halter, rope-blistered hands, and a bruised arm.

"I knew it!" said Farmer Perkins. "Knew it the minute I see them ears. He's a vicious brute, that colt, but we'll tame him."

So four of them, variously armed with whips and pitchforks, went down to the pasture and tried to drive Blue Blazes into a fence corner. But the colt was not to be cornered. From one end of the pasture to the other end he raced. He had had enough of men for that day.

Next morning Farmer Perkins tried familiar strategy. Under his coat he hid a stout halter and a heavy bullwhip. Then, holding a grain measure temptingly before him, he climbed the pasture fence.

In the measure were oats, which he rattled seductively. Also he called mildly and persuasively. Blue Blazes was suspicious. Four times he allowed the farmer to come almost within reaching distance only to turn and bolt with a snort of alarm just at the crucial moment. At last he concluded that he must have just one taste of those oats.

"Come coltie, nice coltie," cooed the man in a strained but conciliating voice.

Blue Blazes planted himself for a sudden whirl, stretched his neck as far as possible, and worked his upper lip inquiringly. The smell of the oats lured him on. Hardly had he touched his nose to the grain before the measure was dropped and he found himself roughly grabbed by the forelock. In a moment he saw the hated straps and ropes. Before he could break away, the halter was around his neck and buckled firmly.

Farmer Perkins changed his tone: "Now, you damned ugly little brute, I've got you!" *(Jerk)* Blast your wicked hide!

(Slash) You will, will you? *(Yank)* I'll larn you!" *(Slash)*

Man and colt were almost exhausted when the "lesson" was finished. It left Blue Blazes ridged with welts, trembling, fright sickened. Never again would he trust himself within reach of those men; no, not if they offered him a whole bushel of oats.

But it was a notable victory. Vauntingly Farmer Perkins told how he had haltered the vicious colt. He was unconscious that a pair of ripe gooseberry eyes turned black with hate, that behind his broad back was shaken a futile fist.

The harness-breaking of Blue Blazes was conducted on much the same plan as his halter-taming, except that during the process he learned to use his heels. One Olsen, who has since walked with a limp, can tell you that.

Another feature of the harness-breaking came as an interruption to further bullwhip play by Farmer Perkins. It was a highly melodramatic episode in which Lafe, gripping the handle of a two-tined pitchfork, his freckled face greenish white and the pupils of his eyes wide with the fear of his own daring, threatened immediate damage to the person of Farmer Perkins unless the said Perkins dropped the whip. This Perkins did. More than that, he fled with ridiculous haste, and in craven terror; while Lafe, having given the trembling colt a parting caress, quitted the farm abruptly and for all time.

As for Blue Blazes, two days later he was sold to a traveling horse-dealer, and departed without any sorrow of farewells. In the weeks during which he trailed over the fruit district of southern Michigan in the wake of the horse buyer, Blue Blazes learned nothing good and much that was ill. He finished the trip with raw hocks, a hoof print on his flank, and teeth marks on neck and withers. Horses led in a bunch do not improve in disposition.

Some of the scores the blue-roan colt paid in kind, some he did not, but he learned the game of give and take. Men and horses alike, he concluded, were against him. If he would hold his own he must be ready with teeth and hoofs. Especially he carried with him always a black, furious hatred of man in general.

So he went about with ears laid back, the whites of his eyes showing, and a bite or a kick ready in any emergency. Day by day the hate in him deepened until it became a master passion. A quick football behind him was enough to send his heels flying as though they had been released by a hair trig-ger. He kicked first and investigated afterward. The sight of a man within reaching distance roused all his ferocity.

He took a full course in vicious tricks. He learned how to crowd a man against the side of a stall, and how to reach him, when at his head, by an upward and forward stroke of the forefoot. He could kick straight behind with lightening quickness, or give the hoof a sweeping side-movement most comprehensive and unexpected. The knack of lifting the bits with the tongue and shoving them forward of the bridle teeth came in time. It made running away a matter of choice.

When it became necessary to cause diversion he would balk. He no longer cared for whips. Physically and mentally he had become hardened to blows. Men he had ceased to fear, for most of them feared him, and he knew it. He only des-pised and hated them. One exception Blue Blazes made. This was in favor of men and boys with red hair and freckles. Such he would not knowingly harm. A long memory had the roan.

Toward his own kind Blue Blazes bore himself defiantly. Double harness was something he loathed. One was not free to work his will on the despised driver if hampered by a pole and mate. In such cases he nipped manes and kicked under the traces until released. He had a special antipathy for gray horses and fought them on the smallest provocation, or upon none at all.

As a result Blue Blazes, while knowing no masters, had many owners, sometimes three in a single week. He began his career by filling a three-months engagement as a livery horse, but after he had run away a dozen times, wrecked several carriages, and disabled a hostler, he was sold for half his purchase price.

Then did he enter upon his wanderings in real earnest. He pulled streetcars, delivery wagons, drays, and ash carts. He was sold to unsuspecting farmers, who, when his evil traits cropped out, swapped him unceremoniously and with ingenious prevarication by the roadside. In the natural course of events he was much punished.

Up and across the southern peninsula of Michigan he drifted contentiously, growing more vicious with each encounter, more daring after each victory. In Muskegon he sent the driver of a grocery wagon to the hospital with a shoulder bite requiring cauterization and four stitches. In Manistee he broke the small bones in the legs of a baker's large boy. In Cadillac a boarding-stable hostler struck him with an iron shovel. Blue Blazes kicked the hostler quite accurately and very suddenly through a window.

Between Cadillac and Kalaska he spent several lively weeks with farmers. Most of them tried various taming

processes. Some escaped with bruises, and some suffered seri-
ous injury. At Alpena he found an owner who, having read
something very convincing in a horse trainer's book, elabo-
rately strapped the roan's legs according to the diagram and
then went into the stall to wreak vengeance with a riding-
whip. Blue Blazes accepted one cut, after which he crushed
the avenger against the plank partition until three of the
man's ribs were broken. The Alpena man was fished from
under the roan's hoofs just in time to save his life.

This incident earned Blue Blazes the name of "man
killer," and it stuck. He even figured in the newspaper dis-
patches. "Blue Blazes, the Michigan Man-Killer," "The
Ugliest Horse Alive," "Alpena's Equine Outlaw"; these were
some of the headlines. The Perkins method had borne fruit.

When purchasers for a four-legged hurricane could no
longer be found, Blue Blazes was sent up the lake to an
obscure little port where they only have a Tuesday and Friday
steamer, and where the blue roan's record was unknown.
Horses were in demand there. In fact, Blue Blazes was sold
almost before he had been led down the gangplank.

"Look out for him," warned the steamboat man; "he's a
wicked brute."

"Oh, I've got a little job that'll soon take the cussedness
out of him," said the purchaser with a laugh.

Blue Blazes was taken down into the gloomy fore-hold of
a three-masted lake schooner, harnessed securely between
two long capstan bars, and set to walking in an aimless circle
while a creaking cable was wound around a drum. At the
other end of the cable were fastened, from time to time,
squared pine logs weighing half a ton each. It was the

business of Blue Blazes to draw these timbers into the hold through a trapdoor opening in the stern. There was nothing to kick save the stout bar, and there was no one to bite. Well out of reach stood a man who cracked a whip and, when not swearing forcefully, shouted "Ged-a-a-ap!"

For several uneventful days he was forced to endure this exasperating condition of affairs with but a single break in monotony. This came on the first evening, when they tried to unhook him. The experiment ended with half a blue-flannel shirt in the teeth of Blue Blazes and a badly scared lumber-shover hiding in the fore-peak. After that they put grain and water in buckets, which they cautiously shoved within his reach.

Of course there had to be an end to this. In due time the *Ellen B.* was full of square timbers. The captain notified the owner of Blue Blazes that he might take his blankety-blanked horse out of the *Ellen B.*'s fore-hold. The owner declined, and entrenched himself behind a pure technicality. The captain had hired from him the use of a horse; would the captain kindly deliver said horse to him, the owner, on the dock? It was a spirited controversy, in which the horse owner scored several points. But the schooner captain by no means admitted defeat. "The *Ellen B.* gets under way inside of a half hour," said he. "If you want your blankety-blanked horse you've got that much time to take him away."

"I stand on my rights," replied the horse owner. "You sail off with my property if you dare. Go ahead! Do it! Next time the Ellen B. puts in here, I'll be liable for damages."

Yet in the face of the threat, the *Ellen B.* cast off her hawsers, spread her sails, and cruised up the lake, bound

Chicagoward through the straits, with Blue Blazes still onboard. Not a man-jack of the crew would venture into the fore-hold, where Blue Blazes was still harnessed to the capstan bars.

When he had been without water or grain for some twelve hours, the wrath in him, which had for days been growing more intense, boiled over. Having voiced his range in raucous squeals, he took to chewing the bridle strap and to kicking the whiffletree. The deck watch gazed down at him in awe. The watch below, separated from him only by a thin partition, expressed profane disapproval of shipping such a passenger.

There was no sleep on the *Ellen B.* that night. About four in the morning the continued effort of Blue Blazes met with reward. The halter-strap parted, and the stout oak whiffletree was splintered into many pieces. For some minutes Blue Blazes explored the hold until he found the gangplank leading upward.

His appearance on the deck of the *Ellen B.* caused something of a panic. The man at the wheel abandoned his post, and as he started for the crosstrees let loose a yell which brought up all hands. Blue Blazes charged them with open mouth. Not a man hesitated to jump for the rigging. The schooner's head came up into the wind, the jib-sheet blocks rattled idly, and the booms swung lazily across the deck, just grazing the ears of Blue Blazes.

How long the roan might have held the deck had not his thirst been greater than his hate cannot be told. Water was what he needed most, for his throat seemed burning, and just overside was an immensity of water. So he leaped. Probably the crew of the *Ellen B.* believe to this day that they escaped by a miracle from a devil-possessed horse who, finding them beyond his reach, committed suicide.

But Blue Blazes had no thought of self-destruction. After swallowing as much lake water as was good for him, he struck out boldly for the shore, which was not more than half a mile distant, swimming easily in the slight swell. Gaining the log-strewn beach, he found himself at the edge of one of those ghostly, fire-blasted tamarack forests which cover great sections of the upper end of Michigan's southern peninsula. At least he escaped from that hateful bondage of man. Contentedly he fell to cropping the coarse beach-grass which grew at the forest's edge.

For many long days Blue Blazes reveled in his freedom, sometimes wandering for miles into the woods, sometimes ranging the beach in search of better pasturage. Water there was aplenty, but food was difficult to find. He even browsed bushes and tree twigs. At first he expected momentarily to see appear one of his enemies, a man. He heard imaginary voices in the beat of the waves, the creaking of wind-tossed treetops, the caw of crows, or in the faint whistlings of distant steamers. He began to look suspiciously behind knolls and stumps. But for many miles up and down the coast was no port, and the only evidences he had of man were the sails of passing schooners, or the trailing smoke-plumes of steamboats.

Not since he could remember had Blue Blazes been so long without feeling a whip laid over his back. Still, he was not wholly content. He felt a strange uneasiness, was conscious of a longing other than a desire for a good feed of oats. Although he knew it not, Blue Blazes, who hated men as few horses have ever hated them, was lonesome. He yearned for human society.

When at last a man did appear on the beach, the horse whirled and dashed into the woods. But he ran only a short distance. Soon he picked his way back to the lake-shore and gazed curiously at the intruder. The man was making a fire of driftwood. Blue Blazes approached him cautiously. The man was bending over the fire, fanning it with his hat. In a moment he looked up.

A half minute, perhaps more, horse and man gazed at each other. Probably it was a moment of great surprise for them both. Certainly it was for the man. Suddenly Blue Blazes pricked his ears forward and whinnied. It was an unmistakable whinny of friendliness, if not of glad recognition. The man on the beach had red hair—hair of the homeliest red you could imagine. Also he had eyes the color of ripe gooseberries.

"You see," said Lafe, in explaining the matter afterward, "I was hunting for burls. I had seen 'em first when I was about sixteen. It was once when a lot of us went up on the steamer from Saginaw after black bass. We landed somewhere and went up a river into Mullet Lake. Well, one day I got after a deer, and he led me off so far I couldn't find my way back to camp. I walked through the woods for more'n a week before I came out on the lake shore. It was a while I was tramping around that I got into a hardwood swamp where I saw them burls, not knowing what they were at the time.

"When I showed up at home my stepfather was tearing mad. He licked me good and had me sent to the reform school. I ran away from there after a while and struck the Perkins farm. That's where I got to know Blue Blazes. After my row with Perkins I drifted about a lot until I got work in this very furniture factory," whereupon Lafe swept a comprehensive hand about, indicating the sumptuously appointed office. "Well, I worked here until I saw them take off the cars a lot of those knots just like the ones I'd seen on the trees up in that swamp. 'What are them things?' says I to the foreman.

"'Burls,' says he.

"'Worth anything?' says I.

"'Are they?' says he. 'They're the most expensive pieces of wood you can find anywhere in this country. Them's what we saw up into veneers.'

"That was enough for me. I had a talk with the president of the company. 'If you can locate that swamp, young man,' says he, 'and it's got in it what you say it has, I'll help you to make your fortune.'

"So I started up the lake to find the swamp. That's how I come to run across Blue Blazes again. How he came to be there I couldn't guess and didn't find out for months. He was as glad to see me as I was to see him. They told me afterward that he was a man-killer. Man-killer, nothing! Why, I rode that horse for over a hundred miles down the lake-shore with not a sign of a bridle on him.

"Of course, he doesn't seem to like other men much, and he did lay up one or two of my hostlers before I understood him. You see—" here Mr. Lafe, furniture magnate, flushed consciously "—I can't have any but redheaded men—redheaded men like me, you know—about my stable, on account of Blue Blazes. 'Course, it's foolish, but I guess the odd fellow had a tough time of it when he was young, same as I did; and now—well, he just suits me, Blue Blazes does. I'd rather ride or drive him than any Thoroughbred in this country; and, by jinks, I'm bound he gets whatever he wants, even if I have to lug in a lot of redheaded men from other states."

GLOSSARY

antiphonal–an antiphon is a psalm or verse sung responsively, however, Twain appears to be using antiphonal to mean "obscure"

asperity–bitterness or sarcasm

backstay–a supporting device at the back of a ship

belay–to secure (as with a rope)

boomers–settlers

bootjack–a device with a V-shaped notch used for pulling off boots

breach–opening or gap

capstan–a machine or device used for moving or raising heavy weights

clandestine–secret or hidden

coulee–a shallow ravine or gully

courser–swift or spirited horse

deadeyes–rounded wood blocks that are encircled by ropes

dory–a flat-bottomed boat with high sides

drummers–traveling salesmen

dunnage–baggage or cargo

effigies–crude figures made to look like someone who is usually hated

effusions–expressions, usually full of feeling

equipage–a horse-drawn carriage

ewed neck–a thin, sloping neck

fetish–an object thought to possess magical powers

fillets–narrow strips of material, or bands

foeman–an enemy in war

furbish–sharpen or polish

gilding–coating or overlaying with gold

goitrous–swollen, especially in the neck area

groundswell–usually spelled out separately (ground swell), this word means a wavelike motion in the ocean caused by a distant gale or storm

hack–a taxi

hawsers–large ropes for towing, mooring, or securing a ship

hippodrome–an arena or stadium used for horse and
  chariot races in ancient Greece
hostler–one who takes care of horses or mules
keelson–a structure running along and above a ship that is
  fastened there to strengthen its framework
leeward–facing in the direction in which the wind is blowing
nimbus–luminous cloud
northers–strong north winds
nuptials–marriage or wedding
porphyrus–purple crystallized
prevarication–falsehood, fib, or lie
progeny–children or offspring
propitious–favorable or lucky
rabble–a disorganized crowd of people, or a mob
ragpicker–an individual who collects scraps for a living
relict–a widow, or something left unchanged
roller–heavy ocean wave
sedentary–settled
sharpers–swindlers
sinuous–crooked or winding
slatted–threw back (as in a horse who threw back his head or
  tossed it around in upset)
soliloquizing–talking to one's self
soothsayers–people said to see into the future
strakes–stripes or bands on a ship's hull
stratagems–plots or plans
swale–a low-lying stretch of land that is often wet
tempests–violent winds
traces–a harness
traps–small carriages
unrequited–not reciprocated or not returned
vanguard–troops moving in the lead
verdant–green
whiffletree–the bar that attaches to the harness and allows a
  carriage to be drawn
yellow lamas–monks or priests dressed in yellow clothing